DARK CONFUSION

A DARK DESIRE SERIES NOVEL

J THOMPSON

Faye.
Meet The enforcers
J Thompson
xxx

USA TODAY BESTSELLING AUTHOR

Copyright © 2021 J Thompson All rights reserved. No part of this book may be used or reproduced in any manner whatsoever without written permission from the author except in the case of brief quotations embodied in articles and reviews.

This book is sold subject to the condition that it shall not, by way of trade or otherwise, be lent, resold, hired out or otherwise circulated without the prior consent of the publisher in any form of binding or cover other than that in which it is published and without a similar condition including this condition being imposed on the subsequent purchaser.

This is a work of fiction. Names, characters, places and incidents are the product of the author's imagination and are used fictitiously. Any resemblance to actual persons, living or dead, business establishments, events or locales is entirely coincidental.

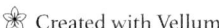 Created with Vellum

ABOUT THE BOOK

Dark Confusion- A Dark Desire Novella.

He had failed.

Callum was one of the best warriors the enforcers had in their ranks, only he felt like a failure. He had failed to protect the one thing that was more important than his own life. She had been taken from him and now he couldn't find her, and he feared the worst. But he wouldn't give up, not when his heart told him she was still alive. He would never give up until he found her, no matter how lost she may seem.

Helena was lost.

Lost to her own mind and to her soul. Since that fateful night she has felt torn, split in half, searching for a way out and the one thing that will complete her and make her feel whole again. Her only problem: she doesn't know what is real or a figment of her imagination. Memories and deep, dark fantasies have merged, making her existence seem like a cruel joke. Can Helena fight the demons within herself? Can she free herself from the prison that is her mind?

1

Mercy: an expensive luxury

"Dammit, get the fucking defibrillator!" the doctor bellowed out in rage as the monitors screamed out a warning that the vitals had flat-lined.

"I want her alive," he yelled out again, his face purple with rage and stress as he started CPR. His meaty hands pressed against the chest of the woman who lay prone on the exam table, her body fully exposed to all as he started a quick rhythm of compressions in the desperate bid to restart the female's heart.

The female, or Subject 12, as the doc had named her, had lasted a lot longer than he had originally expected. When they had first picked her up, he had been convinced she was just another normal human female - until they had started the testing. She had been able to withstand high amounts of pain and had shown accelerated healing. He had also found that - when she had been in the testing room - any males in her vicinity had become affected by her presence. Either she had bewitched his men or she gave off some sort of pheromone, similar to that of a wolf when ready to mate. This had been the first breakthrough since they had acquired her.

She was clearly non-human, but what she actually was, was still unknown. He felt desperate to know how she had come to be in London. He had also become obsessed with Subject 12, but had managed to hide it from the others. As far as they were concerned, he enjoyed inflicting pain upon the creature. He did - to an extent - but he also craved being in her presence.

His mistake now had been pushing her to the limit, even though her body had long ago stopped healing. Her once flawless skin and body now held reminders of all the damage he had personally inflicted. The last bout of electrotherapy had caused her to suffer a bleed on the brain. A grand mal seizure swiftly followed which, in turn, sent her into cardiac failure. He now battled to keep her heart pumping - to keep her alive.

He already missed her unusual pale blue eyes - a feeling he had noticed immediately when she had failed to respond - that and the sparkle and fire that accompanied those orbs. He enjoyed riling her up and watching them burn. But now her eyes were closed, her skin held a blue tinge as her body slowly shut down.

The doc started to panic.

"Breathe, you bitch. Breathe!" he growled out as he continued the compressions, her body twitching with every brutal shove downwards on her chest. It pissed him off more that the other men in the room did nothing to help. Even though he had shouted to have the defibrillator brought to him, they had not moved. All they did was watch.

His arms were getting tired but he wouldn't give up.

There was so much he didn't know about this stunning creature; death would not stop his research. His thoughts drifted to the progress he could still make if he was not able to revive her. Her corpse may just offer the answers he needed and craved.

Could he dissect her body, though?

A sudden single beep brought him out of his musings. He eyed the heart rate monitor and watched as a single blip fired, then another. With a grin, he stopped the compressions and grabbed another syringe, quickly injecting the adrenaline into her body. He felt the needle slide into her sternum as he plunged it directly into her heart.

Her skin slowly returned to its pale pink tone and her chest moved, although, he would have missed it if he hadn't have been watching her so closely.

The doc wiped a clammy hand down his sweat-drenched face and breathed a sigh of relief. He may be a torturing bastard - her words - but he had dreaded stripping her body. This creature - as demonic as his faith implied her to be - was far too beautiful to die.

He knew he was contradicting himself, his own beliefs told him that something like this creature shouldn't even exist and was the work of the devil. But he had always been a bit of a rebel.

The doc, after one long, slow perusal of the creature's body, pulled a sheet to cover her. Yes, he may torture her, mutilate her body just to watch it heal, but it was for scientific purposes and would change the course of human evolution.

"She back with us then, Doc?" one of the men called out, edging closer to the exam table; another male that had become more than a little fond of Subject 12.

The doc nodded in response as he touched her newly

shaven head. He remembered fondly her long raven hair that would cascade over the edge of the table. That first time he had brought her in, it had swept across the floor. No matter how many times they had cut her hair, it had always grown back, although it would now take a while for it to return to its previous splendour. He put that down to the same issue that was stopping her from healing. She had responded well to the drugs they had given her, and even better was her reaction to a liquid form of Viagra they had introduced. The doc had never in his life seen a woman react like that, even in the throes of passion. It was a vision he would never forget and had kept him company on many a lonely night.

"She is back. We will need to be vigilant next time, we were lu-" His words were cut short as the doors to the exam room were thrown open, the force so great it took them clean off the hinges. Five males - all taller than the doc's own guards - stalked in, each holding a weapon. The doc blinked - was that a sword?

His guards looked sluggish and unskilled as the males walked into the room, one large male heading straight towards his new position - knelt behind the exam table. The doc's own heart was ready to stop as the tip of a sword was placed at his throat.

"Stand." The male's voice was low and laced with anger as the doc stood on trembling legs. He pushed the doc backwards until his back hit the counter. The doc focused on the male until he heard a loud growl. Another male, just as large and heavily armed, had stopped by Subject 12's table. The male's eyes roamed over her covered form and forced a jealous response from the doc.

"Don't touch her!" he shouted out, only to have his words cut as the blade pressed harder into his jugular, the skin easily pierced by the blade. The doc felt a small trickle of his blood slide down his throat.

The other male ignored the doc as he bent his head to that of Subject 12's. His whispered words - still loud enough for the doc to hear - shocked him. They were here for her.

"Helena, my love."

The male stroked her cheek and then ran a hand over her shaved head. A look of mortification flickered across his face before he schooled his features. His gaze moved back to stare at her unconscious face with a look of adoration before he lifted the sheet to examine her naked form and the damage the doc had wrought. The doc felt like hours had passed before he was finally pinned with a look filled with so much hate, the doc's heart missed a beat and a feeling of dread swept through his body.

"Did you do this?" the male ground out as he took a step closer, his hands flexed and his eyes blazing, their colour mesmerising.

"Did you?" he asked again, and the doc could do nothing with the sword at his throat but nod. "You will fucking die for what you have done, you and those that serve you!"

Another male stepped forward and stopped the large, angry male from advancing. The doc had a moment of relief before the sword edge was replaced by a large hand that gripped his throat and slowly tightened.

"Callum, stop, we will deal with this, with all of it. Your bonded needs you."

The male dragged his gaze from that of the doc's and stared at the male that had stopped him before he looked back at Subject 12. Acceptance on his face, he nodded. "You will do this for me, Sebastian? You will make this right?"

"Yes, I swear it." The second male, right hand clenched

into a fist, pressed it to his heart and nodded. A bond; a promise.

The male nodded and turned back to the female. The doc knew there and then that he had been dismissed from the male's thoughts instantly; a forgotten memory. The male walked to the table. He took a small blade from a belt that criss-crossed across his torso and swept the edge over his lower lip. The blood instantly bloomed and dripped down his chin. He then bent and pressed his lips to that of the female, forcing them open slightly.

The doc watched, stunned as Subject 12 responded instantly; her arms winding around the neck of the male. Without breaking contact, the male collected her - sheet and all - into his arms, forcing his lips away so he could navigate the room. The doc looked his last at the female before she was carried out of the exam room, and out of his life.

The doc - so engrossed on the response of Subject 12 - missed the movement of the other four males until he stood surrounded. Not one looked capable of giving any mercy.

It was then he knew - knew for sure - that this was his end.

The words of Subject 12 ran through his mind. She had been right all along.

He would die and he would not receive one ounce of mercy.

2

HELENA
A Damsel in distress

Drip...Drip... Drip...

Helena focused on the continual drip of water that echoed nearby. She had yet to open her eyes but the smell of damp stuck into her nose. That - along with the persistent pounding in her head - told her that when she opened her eyes, she most definitely wouldn't be at home. Helena slowly turned her head as she forced her eyes open and groaned as the harsh light caused them to burn. She lifted a hand to cover her eyes as she used her other hand to push herself up on the bed. Her body ached and her head swam so much she nearly fell back down on the musty camp bed she had been dumped on. Nausea rolled through Helena and she fought the need to be sick, instead, wrapping her arms around her middle and looking around.

She had been lying on a small camp bed with only a thin blanket and scrawny pillow that had been placed next to the wall, with head at the end of the room. There was only one exit: a large metal door. Its small window reminded her of those that were shown in prison movies; it could be opened to peek into the room or to give food. But right now it was closed. On the opposite side of the room was a small red bucket, its position answered the question about the ever present drip of water that came from a broken pipe high up in the ceiling. The colour was dreary, reminding her of the bleak stone that surrounded the burial grounds of her kind. A reminder of death.

That summed up her accommodation; a bed and a bucket. If she hadn't have felt so sick, she would have laughed at the ridiculousness of it all. Her thoughts sobered as memories of her abduction flashed back through her mind.

Her last minute trip to the surface, without a chaperone, in the bid to buy Callum a gift, trying to get back to the portal as quickly as she could, only to turn down the wrong alley and find herself surrounded.

Helena shuddered as she remembered the feeling of a heavy weight connecting with her skull before darkness had overtaken her.

She heaved as tears started to fall from her eyes. Ignoring her aches and overall dizziness, she dived for the bucket, only just making it as she emptied her stomach into the plastic receptacle. Her body purged itself of the toxins she had been pumped full of whilst she had been unconscious, until there was nothing left and only dry heaves remained.

The floor was like ice that seeped through her long skirt and thin blouse, despite the fact it was June. It had been a good 25 degrees where she had been in London, and she didn't think she had been held captive so long for the seasons to have changed.

Wiping her mouth on the back of her blouse, she pressed her back into the wall and wrapped her arms around her knees. She had no idea why she had been taken. She had been warned time and time again not to leave the safety of Helvetia, but she had been desperate to go and get a gift that her future bonded would like.

Helvetia was the realm most immortals had been banished to centuries before when the humans turned and started hunting down anyone they classed as unusual. The 'witch trials' were just a cover for the capture and murder of many creatures. So, to protect their species, they went underground. That was the term they used, but to be more accurate, they made a home in a different dimension, which could only be accessed by portals. These portals were placed under most of the major churches in London and other major cities. It had been the creator's way of having a laugh at the humans' expense. They hunted and tortured every creature they deemed evil by their faith, so we hide within the very shadows of the house they deem to be pure.

Most of the races had lost half their numbers, so they all agreed to try and live in Helvetia together, each having their own space and running their own portals. Helena sighed and turned her cheek onto her knee. She should never have left without an enforcer, but there had not been an attack for years, from either humans or another race.

Lifting her right hand, she twisted her palm in the light. The faint scarring shimmered, showing the intricate pattern that had been placed there as a sign that she had been promised. It would only darken to an intense black if she went through a taking ceremony with her bonded - the male meant to be hers for as long as her life permitted.

Her thoughts quickly turned to Callum - an enforcer. He was also the male she had been promised to at infancy. She had known from the first time she had seen him that he would be her mate. Typically, he hadn't been that keen. But as they had grown older together, it had become something they had both wanted.

As a Succubi female, she would need to be bonded before she became sexually mature, as it was only the blood and touch of her male that could control her needs and urges. Unchecked, a female could go on a sexually charged rampage, causing havoc among males, no matter the species. Human males were the most susceptible and could easily be killed and drained of energy. It was only the males of her own kind that had the power to calm and control.

The loud clang of metal on metal sounded and pulled Helena from her thoughts. Squeezing her knees into her body more, she lifted her head and watched as a short male entered the room. He wore a stereotypical white lab coat, large thick-rimmed glasses and had balding hair, thin on top with wisps at the side. To most, his easy smile would be seen as a kindly feature, but to Helena, it sent the warning bells in her head into overdrive. He approached slowly then bent his knees, squatting down next to her so he was closer to her eye level. She couldn't help the shudder that swept through her body as he slowly perused her, taking in every feature. She felt like an insect under a microscope. He smiled wider as she tried to back away further, like she was trying to get inside the wall. Her body felt unresponsive and sluggish and her head still felt muggy.

"Where am I?" she asked, her voice a lot stronger than she thought it would be. "What have you done to me?"

The doc - as she would call him - eyed her before he stood back up and placed his hands into the pockets of his white coat.

"My dear, welcome to The Vault. This is a small facility, as it were, that caters to special people." He paused and smiled again, stepping even closer to her. His eyes paused on the bucket that was now filled with vomit. He didn't seem disgusted with it, but rather, he took the information in and stored it for a later date.

"Edwin, please come and remove this bucket, this can't be pleasant for our guest to have to see," he called out and moved the bucket, with his foot, towards the door, letting the continuous drip of water now hit the floor next to where Helena sat. The sound as it hit the stone floor was dull compared to the sound of it hitting the bucket, but it still felt too loud to her senses, even though they felt dulled.

"You are here, my dear, because you are special."

"I'm not, I'm just an ordinary girl," Helena fired back, determined to reveal nothing of what she was. Humans - as she had been taught - were not to be trusted.

"Ha, there is nothing ordinary about you, my dear," he said. His voice seemed almost elated as he once again bent down and held out a hand, palm up. "Come, let's get you off the floor."

Helena eyed his hand and then his face, not sure what he wanted. She would only admit to herself that she was aching and cold and wanted off the floor. Tentatively, she reached out with her right hand and placed it within his. He smiled gently as he tugged her into a standing position.

"See, that's not too bad," he said and moved with her, out of the corner of the room. Helena couldn't stop the trembling that overtook her now that she was standing.

"There, there, this will help," she heard his voice say

before another pair of hands held her shoulders. "Keep still, I wouldn't want to mark that pretty skin. Well, not yet, anyway," the doc said, a smile on his lips as he pulled a metal syringe from his coat pocket. He uncapped the needle and pulled at her arm.

Helena tried to fight off the hands that held her, only to find another male had moved to her back, stopping any form of escape. He wrapped his muscled bulk around her in a bid to stop her from moving. She again tried to fight but she found she had no strength. She poured everything she had left into head-butting the one behind her and was rewarded with a cry of pain, but not the loosening of his vice-like grip, he only tightened his hold.

"Keep her still, please, Bruce. I can't do this with all the shaking she is doing. That was a good shot, though, Bruce. I will give her that."

Helena then felt the arms that had wrapped around her, tighten further until she could barely breathe, never mind move. She watched as the needle was placed at the crook of her right elbow, and with no skill, the needle pierced her skin. She cried out from the pain of the needle and then the fire that burned up her arm.

Her vision once again swam as whatever had been injected into her system took effect, her mind becoming a foggy mess of memories and flashbacks.

"Hold her, Bruce. We don't want her hurting herself by hitting the floor. Now wait; what is this?" she heard the doc say as she felt fingers trace her right hand, and her bonding mark. As his touch flickered over the scars from her choosing ceremony, she felt a feeling of repulsiveness before her mind sunk into oblivion and her heart called out to her mate.

3

THE VOICES HELP, THE VOICES UNDERSTAND.

"Helena...Shhh, it's ok."

Callum's voice drifted into her mind. The husky tone made her shiver, along with the ghostly touch of his fingers on her skin. She squeezed her eyes shut, trying to keep the dream constant, knowing that as soon as she let go, even a touch, her dream world would vanish and she would be back in the hell-hole prison that had been her home for the past month.

If she concentrated hard enough, she could feel his lips on her forehead as he tried to wake her from her dream. Only, she knew this Callum wasn't real. In her dream, they lay on his huge king-size bed, the soft cotton sheets caressed her skin as she moved and she breathed in deep of a scent that was only Callum, vanilla with a hint of cinnamon. With it it brought the sense of home. She snuggled into his broad chest as he wrapped both arms around her, holding her close.

"I've got you, Helena, and I won't let you go." His voice was deep but quiet and she clutched at the dream, willing it to remain. His presence - although fantasy - made her feel safe and protected. Helena was afraid, afraid of what would happen and if she would, in fact, survive to see her mate again.

Would she have the strength to endure?

"Helena, you are the strongest woman I know. Fight, baby."

His voice vanished and with it, the dream. Helena opened her eyes and fought to hold back the sobs that threatened to overtake her. She let all the pain go with each silent tear and a new determination filled her. She would fight. She wouldn't let them win, and she would see Callum again.

Helena wiped her eyes and sat up. She still felt groggy from the current round of treatment she had been subjected to, but her body seemed to be adjusting. She had accelerated healing from her succubi DNA, which meant the toxins would only affect her fully, once. After that, her body would become immune and fight them off. Helena cradled her hands, gently rubbing them against each other. They still hurt after the doc and his guards had tried breaking her fingers to see how much pain she could actually take.The doc seemed to take great pleasure in each and every scream of pain that he pulled from her. She had once tried to use her succubi gifts to make him stop, but that had ended in a severe beating when they had noticed something was different. Luckily, they still had no clue what she was, but that just meant they would try more and more ways to find out.

Getting to her feet but unable to keep still, Helena began pacing around her small room and started to hum. This had become a habit, since she had been taken. Only, more recently, it had become a way to keep her sane. She had started to hum the tunes to some of the humans' cartoon programmes, and for some unknown reason, it annoyed the hell out of the guards that were seated just down the hall.

Today's anthem was the world famous *Wombles of Wimbledon,* and she couldn't help the smirk that crossed her face as she hummed even louder and was rewarded by cursing from down the corridor. That was one thing they had been allowed to see in Helvetia, they had streamed all of the humans' TV shows as well as their movies. Especially when some of the stars were immortal as well.

The pacing, teamed with the constant drip of the broken water pipe and her humming, made a cacophony of sound that made the dank interior of her cell seem a little bigger.

"Shut the fuck up, bitch, before we shut you up."

Helena walked over to the door of her cell and peeked out the now open trap door that was used to look in on prisoners and slide food into. "Now, now, you know the doc doesn't want me hurt," she called back.

She knew she was playing with fire, but she had to fight, even if it was only by being mouthy to the guards who could and would punish her far more than she was capable of taking.

"He won't mind a few extra bruises." The loud words held a deadly undertone that Helena knew all too well, and her heart plummeted as she saw the owner of the voice she could never forget, step into her view. His name was Bruce, and he was the most brutal of all the guards. He offered a sadistic smile as he came to a stop in front of her door.

"Been crying again, princess?" he sniggered out. "Awwwww, you missing your Callum?" he teased. Helena felt her blood start to boil. They taunted her all time and she always reacted. Callum was her weakness and she couldn't stop herself from taking the bait. The medication they had been forcing her to take every day, had many negative side effects. They were affecting her succubi senses and abilities. But even more alarming is they were causing her to talk in her sleep, baring her most private thoughts about her feelings for Callum, which they often taunted her with later.

"You know, Callum will have moved on by now, princess. He will be banging someone prettier by now. Besides, he's probably some pigeon-chested toddler, anyway." Bruce laughed and peered into the cell. "Just face it, you ain't ever going anywhere."

Helena looked Bruce in the eye and smiled back. He would not wind her up this time, so she kept her reply simple, "Fuck you, lurch."

"That's not very lady like, is it?"

Helena turned her back on the guard and walked back to her bed. Sitting down on the filthy mattress, she let her thoughts turn to revenge. What she would do to Bruce and the doc if she got free, what pain she would exact on them.

Lying back down, Helena grinned and closed her eyes as torture upon torture idea came to mind, giving her something else to focus on.

She would get free.

She had to.

4

WHERE THERE'S PAIN, THERE'S MORE PAIN

Beep...Beep...Beep...

"Helena, baby, wake up." Callum's whispered words forced Helena's consciousness back from the darkness she had been thrust into and returned her to a world of pain and agony.

Beep...Beep...Beep...

The constant beeping penetrated her skull first, and then the pain overtook her body, forcing it to arch on the cold metal table as a scream ripped from her throat.

Everything hurt, not just an ache like when your muscles had been overworked, but a searing pain that boiled and rolled through her. She forced her eyes open as cries continued to fall from her throat and was faced with the smirking face of the doc.

"She's back. Phew! That one was close. Sweetheart, please try not to do that again. Ideally, I need you alive."

Her chest heaved as she forced oxygen in and out of her lungs, although it hurt. Her eyes quickly took in everything, not sure how she had gone from dozing on the camp bed to being strapped naked to an exam table. Her body was exposed for all to see, but when she looked down, expecting to see her pale skin, she saw a gaping hole in her stomach.

"Wha-What have..." She couldn't finish the sentence as the pain flowed through her once again.

"Oh, that. " The doc smiled again and moved down the table before he pulled at an instrument protruding from her body. Instantly, Helena felt sick as a wave of pain coursed through her, so painful she nearly blacked out.

"I was just doing some exploratory surgery when your blood pressure dropped so low you almost flat-lined. So we had to bring you out of anaesthesia. I'm thinking we will have to finish this with you awake." He paused and turned to collect a few more instruments before he turned back and bent close to her. "This may hurt, try not to move too much."

Helena closed her eyes and clenched her teeth together as he continued to mess with her internal organs - pulling and prodding. As screams tore from her throat Helenas only thought was of death, of being allowed peace and a pain free existence. But she knew no matter how hard she begged, it would be futile. That was one request the doc would never agree to. The pain continued to flow through her body, making muscles and nerves twitch in response, until Helena couldn't take any more and she let sweet oblivion take her.

"Come on, baby, you've slept enough." His voice calmed every nerve, muted the pain and soothed her soul. There would be nothing better than to wake up to Callum and know he was real.

"Helena, I know you can hear me." Her fantasy mate wrapped his arms around her and pulled her close to his hard body, his fingers stroking the skin of her bare arms. She felt them move to her hand and to the mark of their bond.

"Soon this will be so dark, there will be no doubt we are bonded, baby. No doubt you are my female."

She wanted to smile at his words, but didn't dare in case the dream vanished, so she stayed still and listened. Callum had never spoken like this in the past, so she would take in the moment and savour it.

"There isn't a place on this earth that I would not follow you, Helena, my love, my bonded."

His words started to fade until the dream had gone, replaced with darkness and silence. But even this was better than The Vault. Anything was better than The Vault.

5

DRIPS AND DARKNESS

Drip...Drip...Drip...

That sound had become almost comforting to Helena, that and the constant voice in the back of her head that reassured her. It was like Callum was with her, helping her through every second of the day, keeping her strong.

Words of love and encouragement helped her deal with some of the horrors the doc would inflict on her. Most of the time she would shout out how much she hated the doc, hated the men that helped him and hated The Vault. She came up with numerous ways they could die for what they were doing to her and the other captives. When Helena wasn't being subjected to the doc's personal attention, she would sit in her cell and listen to the others call out for help or scream into the night as the effects of whatever they had been given, took effect.

The frequency in which new captives appeared should

have concerned Helena, but she had long stopped caring about anything.

She looked at her fingernails - or what was left of them - as she sat cross-legged on her bed. She had awoken this time to find each nail had been removed and all she was now left with were blood-coated, bare nail beds. Every movement of her fingers caused them to throb and ache, but what caused her the most concern was after what felt like most of the day, they were still bleeding.

She had started to notice small changes within her body a few weeks back, but now she had noticed that her usual immortal healing abilities seemed to have stopped. She now bore scars of the doc's cruel treatment and her body retained every agonising muscle memory of the enjoyment he took out on her.

It had been months since she had been clean. The doc liked to keep her in a permanent state of discomfort, which included no showers as well as minimal food and medical treatment. Her long dark hair felt matted. She had tried to contain the locks by braiding it, but every time she came back from being "treated", it was loose. The doc had started to display more and more obsessive behaviour towards her, but had also started to become more brutal with his treatments.

Helena had lost weight since she had been taken and she knew if she looked into a mirror, she wouldn't recognise herself. She would be surprised if anyone would.

She had once been curvy. That was one of the things Callum used to mention when he held her in his arms: that he adored each and every one of her lush curves; that they were made to fit his hands alone. Now he would look at her and see only a shell of the woman she was, be repulsed by the new scar that now bisected her torso. She may have woken up this time with bleeding nails, but the memory of the pain she had been in before darkness had taken her was fresh in her mind. To look down your body and see your internal organs being moved and prodded... The physical and psychological pain had been indescribable. She had blacked out not long after.

Helena lifted her blouse to look at the raw wound. Large, ugly staples held her skin together, but blood still seeped slowly from it, soaking into her blouse. It caused a constant throb, and whatever the doc had done on the inside hurt even more.

"Shhhh, Helena, baby, I got you." Callum's whispered voice filtered through her mind. To her, it sounded like it filled the small cell, but she knew she was the only one that could hear it. Tears collected in her eyes and slid down her cheek as she tried, with everything she had, to hold on to the fantasy of him.

"I can't last much longer, Callum. They are killing me," she whispered back as she curled into a ball on the camp bed. She looked at her palm, her bloody fingers tracing the pattern.

"Baby, you can and you will. I've got you and I won't let you go." His voice soothed only a fraction of her soul. Her heart ached, a pain that was nearly as bad as the physical.

"Callum, I love you. I don't want to die here." Helena sobbed on her words as her body started to shake. She could feel her body going into shock and she went with it. Maybe now she would get peace.

"I'm coming, baby, I've got you." Callum's calm voice caressed her mind as Helena did the one thing she knew would allow her to escape, if only for a short while.

She let darkness take her.

6

DIGNITY THERE, DIGNITY GONE...AND MY SOUL

"Helena," he called out again. Helena wanted to answer but found she couldn't - her voice wouldn't work. Inside, she called Callum's name, begging him to not leave her. To save her from the nightmare her existence had become. But every time she felt she was getting closer to his voice, it would vanish completely.

Helena craved oblivion. She yearned for the weightlessness and pain-free existence that only oblivion could offer.

"Helena." His voice sounded again before it drifted away on a whisper, her hope seeming to go with it. Callum would not rescue her, no one would. Helena had finally accepted that, but she would never show how hopeless she actually felt, not to the doc. That man preyed and focused on weakness. He hunted out hers and if he found them all, he would destroy her.

"Subject 12." The doc's cold voice, devoid of feeling, penetrated the fog of unconsciousness that she had been cocooned within. It dragged her back to reality and back to a nightmare full of pain.

"Wakey, wakey, sweetheart." Helena blinked before squeezing her eyes shut again as the bright light from above, burned into her retinas, the searing pain bringing her to full consciousness.

"That's it. It's about time you woke up. I need you bright as a button today. We have lots of fun planned."

Adjusting to the light, Helena slowly opened her eyes to find the doc's face looming over her. It was a face she had come to loathe. Everything, from his pale eyes, to his balding hair and tea-stained teeth, set her on edge. This time he had a grin on his face, a grin that sent a shiver up her spine.

"Ahh, that's good, we like to see those beautiful eyes of yours."

Helena's gut tightened as hatred for this man filled her. She had never been a violent person; she had been brought up away from the violence of her kind. When she looked back on her life - as short as it was - she realised she had been sheltered. Not only from the human world, but also the immortal domain where she had resided.

Her kind, by the order of the high counsellor, Michael, had been banned from any travel to the human domain without the protection of an enforcer. It had been his way of "protecting" their kind, yet it felt more like he was trying to restrict anything they did. He had demonstrated his force as a leader by stopping all bondings that were usually arranged at birth. This had been the tradition for their kind since records had begun. Initially, Helena and many others had thought this would be ok for their kind, that they were moving with the times and transitioning into the modern world. But before she had taken her regretful trip, there had been whispers of Michael now forcing bondings in an attempt to keep the bloodlines pure.

Michael had taken leadership of the succubi council when their queen had vanished - along with her only daughter - only hours after news of the queen's consort being killed in a conflict with the vampyres. Talk and rumour had been rife that Michael had planned it all along, but his support outweighed that of any competition.

Helena had never taken an interest in politics but, from her simple point of view, the force of any bond between the males and females of her kind would only end in disaster, and that alone did not bode well for the future of her race.

Her thoughts of her kind made her heart ache. She missed everything, including her minder, Mirium, who, when Helena's parents had died at the age of six, had taken her in and raised her. That woman had been one of the only people Helena had cared about. Mirium and Callum had been her world - they still were - and it hurt to think she had caused them so much pain, all because of a silly trip to the surface. She hated to think she had inflicted pain on anyone, not when she now had an up close and personal experience with that demon itself.

"Right, my dear." The doc's voice, laced with excitement, grated on Helena's nerves. Her fingers twitched as she imagined wrapping them around his delicate human neck and squeezing. Her fingers were about all she could move. After her last bout of treatment, he had taken an obvious liking to strapping her down. This time, though, he had added more straps. They held her head, biceps, wrists, thighs and ankles, with one more placed across her hips. She had tried to move a few times since she had woken, but it was no use. Every time she moved even an inch, the thick leather straps rubbed against her skin, creating more and more bruises to add to the already large collection.

"Today's fun starts with this." The doc smiled rather sadistically as he held up a large syringe. The liquid inside was clear, but the excitement in the doc's eyes and exaggerated movements told Helena she would not enjoy this nearly as much as he would.

She struggled against the straps, ignoring the pain they caused as they cut into her skin. She had to fight. Her mind may have nearly lost hope, but her body hated every second he had her locked up. There was still a small voice in her thoughts that would not let her totally give in.

"My dear, when will you learn not to fight, can't you see it's pointless?"

"Go to hell," Helena spat out and followed it with a glare, pouring every bit of hate she felt into it. If she had the bodily fluids, she would have spat in his face. His answer was to smile before walking to the end of the exam table, close to her feet. Helena's body was not naked this time, but covered with a small paper smock that barely covered her breasts and torso. She missed her skirt and blouse. Hell, she missed being clean; missed her bed, missed everything she had before this monster had taken her away.

Helena tensed as she felt the doc's fingers whisper over the skin of her upper thigh. The way her legs had been strapped down meant they had been placed slightly apart, leaving her exposed for the entire room to see. His hand lingered on her right upper thigh, almost caressing in his manner, which caused Helena to once again attempt to move.

"Get off me," she screamed, her heart rate spiking as panic started to set in.

In all the other tests, the doc had aimed his focus on her

tolerance to pain as well as trying to figure out what she was. Now, his focus has shifted and Helena felt sick. She was still a virgin, as was custom for her kind before she entered into the taking ceremony. The ceremony would always take place before the female would hit maturity.

Helena cried out as she felt every centimetre of the long needle he pressed none too gently into the artery of her inner thigh. The liquid burned as it entered her bloodstream, forcing another cry of pain from Helena's lips. The doc's hand on her thigh was soon forgotten as heat - intense heat - erupted and travelled through her body.

"Ok, Subject 12 has been injected with a liquid form of Sildenafil Citrate. This is a concentrated form of the Viagra drug which has been mixed with a combination of other drugs specified in my notes. I have injected directly into the femoral artery for a more intense and rapid reaction. Subject did seem a little more panicked than usual today. Straps have been used to hold her in place and to save her from injury. I have noted again that her stomach wound from our last inspection had not healed as it should, even by human standards, and there seems to be a small infection brewing."

Helena tried to fight the doc, but she couldn't move. He checked her pulse and then her eyes, all the while talking into his tape recorder.

"Eyes seem paler than usual and are now fully dilated, heart rate had spiked. The body seems to be reacting as expected and there is an odour of vanilla that is now present within the room. I have noticed that this same odour was present not long after we first collected Subject 12."

Helena couldn't concentrate on the doc as her body reacted violently to the drugs. She had only briefly heard of Viagra from the guards when they had been discussing what had been done to another prisoner, this one a male. She knew what they had given her and it scared her more than any of the other tests they had performed.

Every muscle in her body twitched, wanting to move but prevented from doing so by the straps that held her down. Helena's head buzzed and her heart beat so fast and hard, she could feel it thump against her rib cage. Her breasts seem to swell and throb. Her nipples - now erect - pressed against the paper smock, and every movement sent shivers up and down her spine. Helena cried out as wave after wave of intense heat flowed through her. Tingles and butterflies erupted within in her stomach as her core throbbed with a need Helena had never felt before. Every beat of her heart, created an answering one down below. The need to press her thighs together - to battle the throb - was almost intolerable and had her crying out as they strained against the straps.

"What did you do to me?" Helena panted as white noise filled her ears and her body felt like it had burst into flames.

The doc ignored her words as he walked around the exam table. Recorder in hand, he was all scientist: detached and cold.

"Subject 12 appears to be reacting positively to the drug. Vitals show an elevated heart rate and she seems unable to remain still. In short, she has all the signs of being sexually aroused."

"WHAT DID YOU DO TO ME?" Helena screamed, her body no longer her own. She watched the doc as he placed the recorder onto a nearby table, before he moved towards the end of the exam table. His now gloved hands again touched her thighs. Helena screamed to fight off both the feeling erupting inside and against his touch, but both went ignored. Against her wishes, every touch both fuelled and calmed the raging inferno that burned through her. For the first time since she had been taken, her succubi senses erupted with full response, the drug counteracting whatever the doc had done to stop them from surfacing, making the transition into full maturity happen in rapid succession.

She could feel her body changing, her gums aching as her new small fangs forced their way through the soft tissues. The need to feed added to the already overwhelming needs that ran riot through her body. Helena had been told about what would happen when she hit maturity, how intense it was and how, when it hit, her male would lead her through the feeding.

In her mind, Helena called out for Callum, called for her mate. She knew what was happening to her and she fought against it. Out of all the torture the doc and his lackeys had put her through - every beating, every wound - was nothing compared to what he was doing to her now. Without realising, the doc was destroying any hope of a future for Helena. He was destroying the sacred bond that would bond her to her mate.

Her body was on the edge of the precipice, ready to tumble and fall at any point. Every essence of her being rebelled, but it would be dragged from her by force. All it would take was one touch, one single touch to lose her soul.

The doc's voice penetrated her fog, her eyes filled with tears as she listened once again to his detached voice. "Subject 12, on examination, is indeed sexually aroused," he said calmly and with detachment as he started the physical exam. His fingers roughly parted her over-sensitive and engorged folds before they penetrated her core.

Helena fought against the impending orgasm, fought with everything she had, but her body wouldn't listen. It was ripped from her, all in the name of research. Her core clamped down on the doc's fingers. She screamed and sobbed as the drug forced it to happen over and over again.

Tears flowed from her eyes as blessed darkness pressed in. Helena called out again, called for Callum, both out loud and in her mind.

"Callum!"

She apologised for letting someone else take from them what should have only belonged to him. Their bond now destroyed, Helena fell into oblivion's sweet embrace.

"Callum…"

7

Strength, I have none.

"Stay strong, Helena."

"Stay strong."

"Stay strong."

Those words repeated over and over in her skull. Callum's voice had become more and more persistent, constantly telling her to be strong. It was easier said than done, though. Helena was unsure she could actually hold on for much longer. The doc had managed to strip her of every ounce of dignity and had destroyed any and all hope Helena had of a future. Because of him, no male would want her, even her Callum. That was even if she ever did escape this hellhole. Because of the doc, she had been pushed through her maturity before she was ready. She had been put through her first climax without her bonded male. That bond was fragile at the beginning, and Helena had no clue how it would now stand. She wouldn't blame Callum - if she ever made it out - if he turned his back on her. What male would want his female as tainted as she was?

"Stay strong. I'm here, my love." His voice rang clear in her mind and Helena shook her head, answering him out loud.

"No! No, Callum, don't you lie to me."

Every inch of her body hurt. The wound on her stomach was now red and inflamed, each staple that had been placed to hold her skin together now oozed with blood and other foul smelling fluids.

After the last test they had done on her sexual response, she had been pumped with a combination of drugs that had done nothing for the pain but made her unable to walk or stand. Her legs felt like jelly on a constant basis and the room constantly spun. She wanted to sleep more than anything, but she was scared to.

So far, every time she had succumbed to a deep sleep, she had been awoken on the exam table, ready to have more tests done in an effort to find out what she was. The doc was obsessed with this question and would repeatedly ask her, knowing she wouldn't say anything. She had become his personal play thing, like a child would catch an insect, slowly removing its wings and pulling its legs off to see how it worked. It was almost as if he was trying to see what made her, her.

When she had been placed in the exam room - before her nails had been removed - she had noted a large cross that hung over the door to the room. The doc was a religious and superstitious man, which explained the mumblings of demon and evil. Yes, she was in fact a demon, but not as he thought. The doc's own mind had become warped in the twisted world he had created for himself, believing his actions in testing creatures like herself, and others, to be the work in the name of whoever he worshipped. When, in fact, he himself was acting more and more like the dark beings that resided deep in the shadows. His belief that he was in the right would be his downfall. She may not be around to see it, but it would happen.

Helena wrapped her arms around her knees and pulled them as close as her inflamed stomach would allow. She winced as waves of pain travelled through her body. Pain had become the norm for her now. If there was ever a time that she wasn't in pain, she would no doubt miss it. Dressed no longer in that small paper smock, Helena wore a thin hospital gown that had seen better days. Its thin fabric did nothing to keep her warm or protected from the cold and damp of her cell, and in her current position, sat in the corner on the cold floor, she may as well have been naked. She had forgotten what is what like to be warm, to be clean. The idea of a bath was a distant memory, like those of Callum.

The cold seeped into her skin, helping her to stay awake. The concrete floor just added to her discomfort, but she had stopped caring. Every now and again, her frail body would go into spasm, the muscles twitching in memory from the onslaught of torture she had been subjected to.

Helena rested her cheek onto her knees as she fought the exhaustion that flowed through her body. She rocked gently, forward and back, and ignored the continual drip of the water into the bucket, the screams of fellow inmates and the usual taunting from the guards.

Callum's voice echoed in her mind, louder than it had ever been before. "Stay strong."

She answered, her eyes glued to the other side of the room. She could almost picture Callum knelt in front of her, his eyes pleading. "I can't, Callum."

"Stay strong," he repeated, his hand reaching out to touch her, but not quite making contact.

"Callum, I can't," she cried out. "I don't want to," she sobbed, letting the tears fall freely. "I want to be free, Callum. I want to rest."

Her voice broke as exhaustion won the battle, 72 hours she had stayed awake, 72 hours she had forced her body and mind to function and deny the doc his chance to take her again. She had fought the drugs they had forced on her, but now, she had little fight left.

"Rest, my love." His voice felt closer, like a caress of her mind and soul. "I've got you."

Closing her eyes, Helena fell willingly into slumber, a dream world filled with light and hope, away from the nightmare of reality.

"Helena! Helena!"

Callum's voice called out from within the woods and she grinned from her hiding place. She pressed herself against the trunk of the huge oak she had chosen as her hiding place, knowing the old tree would hide her presence. She hoped that he wouldn't find her and in the same thought, she couldn't wait until he did.

With only a few weeks left until they were to be bonded, Callum had surprised her by sneaking them both out of the realm without a chaperone. Usually, an enforcer counted as one, unless you were soon to be joined, then it was frowned upon. Amazing how their race had come leaps and bounds in technology, yet still required unmated females to be chaperoned.

Callum called it private time for them, even though Helena was positive that they would have plenty of that after the ceremony.

Helena grinned and covered her mouth to hide the sound of a giggle that sneaked its way out of her lips. She knew even the slightest sound would be heard by Callum, and then he would find her. He was, after all, one of the best warriors in the alpha team of the enforcers and had been recruited as such, as soon as he had finished his training. She couldn't have been prouder of her male, but since he had been made a part of the team, it felt, to Helena, like she was losing him. His attention always seemed elsewhere when they were together. His visits had also become less frequent and had her questioning whether he had wanted to be bonded after all. He would be the only one in the alpha team that was. To most, that would seem lucky, but the whispers she had heard was that most of the males preferred to be unbound. Helena had been convinced that he would call off the ceremony, that was until he had left her a note and arranged this trip.

Helena leaned back against the rough bark of the oak tree and closed her eyes, almost holding her breath, attempting to stay as silent as she possibly could. Her heart thundered in her chest with excitement and her palms became sweaty as they pressed against the bark. In seconds, the air around her changed, becoming heavy and intense. Helena kept her eyes closed, already knowing that Callum had found her. His musky scent enveloped her senses and swept over her in a way she would never get tired of. His whispered breath sounded in her ear.

"Found you."

Her breath hitched and goosebumps erupted all over her skin. With only a few words, this male seemed to always have a way to make her breathless and weak at the knees. He had done since the first time she had been able to understand her feelings. As a child, he was her best friend, but as they had grown, she had known he would belong to her and she would to him.

"Open those beautiful eyes, baby," he said quietly as his lips ghosted over her own, his sweet breath filling her senses.

Helena did as she was commanded, her pale orbs meeting his dark ones. Callum had caged her in against the trunk of the tree, his muscled arms offering shelter and protection. She never once felt trapped. She took in every part of his face. His chiselled perfection, slightly crooked nose and tousled hair that fell over his eyes, made her heart ache. But what made her heart beat harder was the look in his dark eyes; a look she knew would be reflected back. She loved this male more than anything else, in this realm or her own.

"That's better, angel." His voice was calm, yet husky, wrapping around her, soothing and coaxing.

"Callum," she murmured on a whispered breath and tilted her head upwards in a silent plea, wanting Callum to kiss her.

"That's my girl," Callum growled out as he moved his right hand from the trunk of the tree and slid it up her arm. His fingers skated over her skin before his hand swept up the column of her throat. Callum's thumb caressed the line of her jaw before his fingers delved into her hair, holding Helena's head in place as he took possession of her mouth. The moment their lips touched, Helena was lost to sensation, lost to the feel of her male as he bent her to his will. His taste became overpowering as his blood filled her mouth. Unable to stop herself, she drank fully, knowing they had gone against tradition, yet elated as this meant they had started the bond that would seal them for all time.

This was her male.
Her hunter.
Her Callum.

8

WHEN WILL IT END, WHEN CAN I REST?

Helena's throat erupted into a scream as she was pulled from the perfection of her dream and back into a nightmare. Freezing cold water coated her completely, waking her in an instant. The laughter of the guards responsible filtered through her fogged mind and made her realise her mistake.

She had fallen asleep again, and in that time the doc had once again managed to drug her and get her back into the exam room with no fight. She was once again strapped down to the table, naked and at the mercy of both the guards and the doc. Her nakedness didn't bother her as much as it used to, her dignity had long since vanished and the drawn out stares of the guards just irritated her when once they would have made her embarrassed.

"Was that little dream a good one?" Bruce, the guard, sneered as he tightened the strap that crossed her torso, his fingers deliberately pressed against her skin. "Missing your dear Callum?" He laughed and slid his hands up her body before squeezing her bare breasts, hard, instantly bringing tears to her eyes.

"He's forgotten you, everyone you knew has." He grinned as he taunted her. He bent his head to her ear, first licking across her cheek and making Helena shudder in repulsion. "No fucker would want you now, anyway. Well, only as a hole."

With his parting shot, he stood and backed away, all the while his grin remained plastered to his face.

"Now, now, Bruce," the doc chided as he turned around to face the table. He had been reading his notes whilst she had been strapped down, his mind on the test yet to come. He treated Helena as if it was her fault that the guards abused her, like this was all her fault.

"My dear, please don't antagonise my men. You are, after all, only a bit of... Oh, what's that phrase, Bruce?" The doc smiled at his men, then remembered, "Oh yes, you are but a piece of tits and arse." To Helena, anything of the vulgar variety that came out of the doc's mouth just sounded wrong in comparison to the guards.

Helena glared at him, but said nothing. Usually, when she reacted, he would make sure her punishment was harsh, but she had become past caring. Her body still retained every scar of what they had done.

"Now, today's fun and games will start with a little shave." The doc smiled as he turned to his tray table and collected a pair of clippers. He approached Helena's head, and all she could do was watch. Her entire body had been strapped down again, so tight she was unable to move. Helena wanted to fight but she had little energy left. Her eyes followed the doc as he shaved the hair around her temples, her long locks falling to the floor in a silken mess.

"Now, don't move, sweetheart. Stay still, I don't want to

have to shave off all of your pretty hair." The doc chuckled as he called out to one of the guards to come and hold her head down. Helena refused to give up the fight, though. She screamed as loud as she could and even tried to bite Bruce. That earned her a smack to the face and Bruce grabbing her by the hair, tugging the strands so hard she felt them rip from her scalp.

"Well, looks as though you want all your hair shaving off. Bruce, you may as well do the honours." The doc chuckled and handed the clippers over to the guard. Helena screamed again, this time in pain as Bruce butchered her scalp with the clippers; not caring if he caught her skin. Out of the corner of her eye, she watched as the silky strands, although matted, drifted to the floor. Tears fell from her eyes, even as the doc then proceeded to lather up her temples with soap. With surgical skill, he made quick work of finishing the shave before putting sticky pads in place. Each had wires attached that went to a machine nearby, as well as pads that were stuck to her throat, right over the carotid artery. The steady beep that filled the room, she now understood was her heartbeat, its sound taunting her almost as bad as the guards.

"What are you doing?" she asked, her eyes darting to and from the doc and the machine that was wheeled closer to her table. The room had grown cold and she felt it to her core. She shivered against the metal table, her fingers making a fist then releasing. She needed to move something; her body was on edge and her mind close to breaking.

The doc's cold voice filled the room as he started to speak into his digital recorder, making her feel once again like a lab rat would feel. "Today's testing will again take place on Subject 12. She has been brought to the exam room after a week. We found she needed time to recoup after the last round of testing, which had positive results. She has been, once again, strapped to the table in the hopes we can prevent any injury. Subject 12 does seem to fight any and all processes."

Helena glared again as he walked the length of the exam table, poking and prodding her injuries as he went, all the while making a verbal note of his deeds. She wanted to shout what a sadistic prick he was, but it would make no difference.

"On examination, Subject 12 is still not healing. Her accelerated healing from when we first brought her in has completely vanished and now she is not even healing like a human. The incision I made across her stomach, although stapled, seems to now be red in colour and when I palpate the soft tissue, blood and what looks like infection material secretes from it."

Helena cried out as the doc, none too gently, pressed each wound, the pain becoming so intense she gagged as nausea tried to take over.

"If all goes well with today's testing, I will proceed to commence treatment for infection with multiple antibiotics. We are still unaware of what Subject 12 actually is, so multiple courses may be needed. However, if the skin starts to necrotize then surgery will be needed to remove the infection manually."

The doc checked the wound on her stomach one last time before he moved away again. Instructing a guard to hold the recorder and to keep it running, he pulled the trolley that held the machine closer, the wires attaching to the pads on Helena's temples. "Today's test will consist of shock therapy. As with the sexual response testing, I am trying to ascertain exactly how much the subject can take. In this case, how much the brain can take. As with all testing there are risks, the possibility of brain damage is high, along with brain bleeds and the onset of seizures." He smiled down at Helena and her gut twisted. Even to her limited knowledge, sending electricity directly into the brain would be unpleasant and would put her through of world of pain. Again.

"Shall we get started?" the doc said in a sing-song voice; the scientist excited and eager to start. Helena moved her head as much as she could in a vain attempt to loosen the straps. The mere thought of what was about to happen gave her a small amount of strength to fight, although it wouldn't be much of a fight.

"Bruce, please come and tighten the straps around her head, I can't afford for her to be thrashing about once the treatment has started."

"You bastard," Helena shouted out, unable to keep her rage locked in. Even when Bruce forced her head down to tighten the straps, she continued to shout at the doc. "You will die, you evil piece of shit, all of you will," she spat out. "You will beg for mercy and none will be given. I hope you rot in hell."

"We shall see, Subject 12, we shall see." With a sadistic smile, the doc nodded to Bruce and the guard stepped away from the table as the doc turned on the machine. A gentle hum filled the room as it warmed up and the doc collected two rods with wires attached and approached Helena's head.

"Test one: electroshock therapy, about to commence." Helena refused to close her eyes. Instead, she glared at the doc, and hatred for this man filled her.

"I hate you," she spat out a moment before the rods made contact with the pads at her temple.

Pain like nothing she had experienced before filled her

mind, ripping her consciousness to shreds. She felt her body buck as the onslaught intensified. Helena closed her eyes but bright lights burst through her eyelids as surge after surge of electricity pulsed through her. She screamed out as her body no longer responded to her commands. Convulsions contorted her and foam formed at her mouth. Her mind fractured, showing her every moment of her life before her abduction. Her heart, although struggling with the overflow of electric current, ached for what could have been with her male. She prayed to whatever god was listening that she would pass over to the other side to await her warrior.

The pain was so intense, Helena let go. Let go of life and of the fight. As wave after wave swept through her, Helena went with it, letting her heartbeat slow until it stopped. She let darkness descend one last time, going with it willingly.

Blessed darkness.
Blessed oblivion.
Blessed death.

9

CALLUM
Enforcers...

The echo of footsteps filled the alley as the males stalked their chosen path, their unit melded into the shadows, unseen by any unsuspecting mortals. Each of the six enforcers had stealth - a skill few could equal - and all had been chosen to form an Alpha team of the most lethal quality. They were the best, they were the deadliest and they had no mercy.

Tasked with the job of protecting their kind, they had all taken the abduction of one of their females as a personal blow. What made the situation even worse was that it was a female belonging to Callum; one of the six enforcers present. Taken only days before their bonding ceremony was due to take place, the loss had hit Callum hard.

Callum and Helena had been one of the last birth pairings to happen within their kind. He felt lucky to have been chosen now, feeling for the younger generation that would not have that in their lives. Forcing couples together, not giving them a chance to bond. Michael, the head of the succubi council, was convinced that this would strengthen their kind when, in fact, it was destroying the succubi breed. Fewer children were being born and more and more females were enduring maturity alone and then going rogue. He was destroying their race one decree at a time. The succubi based their existence on the bond formed at birth with their chosen. It was a sacred trust that few other races would understand.

It was obvious to most that Michael cared only for himself and the power he had gained and wielded over the race. There was little they could do at the moment, other than watch and wait. Only the return of the true monarch would give them a chance at surviving.

10

Hunting...Killing...My job.

Callum stopped in his tracks as Dominic held up a fist, the silent signal told them they were close. It had taken months to get this far, so they had to be careful, it would take only one single mishap and the mission could be ruined.

Callum moved forward, silently passing the other males as he waited for Dominic, their leader, and one of the most powerful enforcers to be born. He had his eyes closed, brows drawn in deep concentration. Dominic had gifts, ones that you didn't question, you just went with, and right now, Callum needed those gifts to be shit hot and on target.

"Dom, you finished meditating yet? I need to piss." Callum glared behind him as the youngest of the group, Cooper, piped up as he leant against the wall, cigarette hanging from his mouth. He was a cocky bastard and usually managed to annoy most of the enforcers all at the same time.

Callum growled as he stalked up to the youngster, ready

to wrap his hand around his throat, only Sebastian blocked his path.

"Callum, no, leave him."

"He needs to shut his fucking mouth, Seb. I won't have him fucking this up, not when we are this close."

Sebastian nodded to Callum before he turned and cuffed Cooper upside of the head, making him cough on his cigarette. "Shut the fuck up, Coop, before one of us shuts you up permanently."

This collection of males had been Callum's family now for many a year, they had formed a bond few teams had, and were feared. The youngest and cockiest being Cooper, who's mouth usually got him into more trouble than was worth. He was tall at near on 7ft, with an easy smile, chocolate brown hair and grey eyes. The next, and probably the quietest warrior, was Stefan. He had come to them from Latvia. He had lost his own bonded mate to an attack by the dark fey and he had gone on a hunting spree, destroying any fey, demon or vampyre he could find. It had only been through the help of Dom that he had come out of his berserker style daze. He had been with them ever since. He had melded into the team, becoming the deadliest male they had. With long black hair, eyes so brown they also looked black, and a build that could rival any fighter, he was solid and pure muscle.

His closest friend from childhood, Alec, had also been chosen for the alpha team. It felt good to have someone he had known since infancy at his back, he also knew how much their current mission meant to him. Alec was a brawler first and foremost, but he also had an incredible talent with a bow and arrow that few could equal. At 6ft 5 he was the shortest of the team, packed with muscle and electric blue eyes. With short brown hair that always looked mussed, he used his good looks and charm everywhere he went.. He also had the best sense of humour going, which helped lighten up some missions. But not this one.

Sebastian was a force to be reckoned with and he looked it. Keeping to the old ways, he kept his light brown hair long and tied back. With an aristocratic face, he looked like he should belong in the royal wing, not fighting on the street. He always took each and every mission personally. Both he and Dominic enjoyed using swords but they weren't averse to using fists. Sebastian had a past, but no one ever asked about it, or asked where his own mate was. With his dark bonding marks, it was obvious he had been bonded at some point.

A loud whistle pulled Callum's attention back to Dom, who's fingers twitched, summoning him over.

"Callum," Dom said, his voice quiet, yet hard. "We go in, all of us."

"This is the place?" Callum asked, his heart beating ten to the dozen. Finally, after months of searching, months of interrogating, it had finally paid off.

"Callum, my friend," Dom's eyes met his own, pity already filled the orbs, "please be prepared for the worst." Callum could only manage a nod as he drew both his daggers from underneath his jacket. He had been prepared for the worst since the day he had been told Helena was missing. At first, he had been convinced it was all his fault. He hadn't been paying her proper attention and had avoided seeing her after missions. It wasn't because he didn't care for her. Hell, he loved that woman with every inch of his soul. He just didn't want to taint something so sure and pure with stories of death and mayhem. Instead, he had stayed with

Dom or Sebastian to wind down and then had gone to see her.

Only after she had been gone had her minder, Mirium, told him that Helena had left the safety of her home and their realm; had gone to the human world for one reason. Guilt ate at Callum when he learned she had felt the need to risk herself for him. She had gone to buy him a gift before they were to be joined. Her kind heart and beautiful soul gone - in the blink of an eye - all because of him.

Each male moved forward, none making a sound as they drew close to the entrance, only to stop mid-stride as a blood curdling scream filled the air. A scream filled with agony, an agony Callum knew deep inside but refused to let anyone see His own heart stopped for a mere second then started straight into a gallop, his mind in denial yet already knowing who the owner of the scream was.

"We go in hard, no mercy. First, we find our target then we free any others." Dominic's voice drilled into the night moments before he bent his head, eyes closed and with immense power, blew the doors to the building open.

11

ONLY A BOND WILL SURVIVE

Callum sheathed both his daggers quickly, before he followed the others through the large metal doors. When they had first blasted through, any guards that had been present had been either killed on impact or knocked unconscious. Only having two guarding the entrance meant Cooper would be bored now from the lack of a fight and they wouldn't hear the end of it.

Beyond the entrance lay a single corridor with multiple doors on each side. On a cursory glance, it was obvious they were cells, some occupied but poor souls that had been tortured to the point of death. What surprised him was that most were human.

One cell in particular called to him, he had walked in and had instantly known his Helena had been kept there. Her scent hung like a cloud, along with the scent of her blood. This had his fists tightening in anger. His keen eyesight noticed the markings on the wall in the corner and had him bending down. Small words had been scratched into the rock and had his heart constricting.

Strong

Callum

Love

These three words had been scratched over and over. His fingers found the small piece of stone that had been Helena's tool. Dried blood coated it from where the sharp points had dug into her skin. Callum stood, pocketing the small rock, he turned and left the cell both eager and dreading what would be found next.

"Alphas," Sebastian called out, summoning them all to another set of double doors at the end of the corridor. "Ready?" he asked and waited for a nod from each male.

Callum watched as both Dominic and Sebastian kicked the double doors open, entering the next room on swift feet, the rest of the men quickly followed. Callum knew the others would disarm any guards as they came face to face with a short balding man over an exam table.

Callum's heart once again stopped as he looked down at the victim of the doctor's mercy. His Helena lay prone on the table, covered in a sheet, her skin unusually pale. Callum approached, his hands shook as he reached out to touch her. Something he thought he would never do again.

"Helena, my love," he whispered out as his right hand lifted and caressed her cheek. He was shocked at how she looked. Her face was sunken, showing defined cheekbones only possible from malnutrition. Her hair was gone, her head shaved clean of the long beautiful locks he had loved braiding.

The sheet that covered her stopped just above her breasts, the skin that was visible was covered in bruises so dark they could have been mistaken for tattoos. Callum brushed his fingers over Helena's bare scalp, gently removing the sticky pads and wires that were attached and then removed the ones on her neck before he went to lift the sheet.

"Don't touch her," the doctor's squeaky voice called out. Callum lifted his eyes to glare at him before he looked down at his mate's naked body. The sheet had hidden the worst of the damage done to her. It made Callum sick to his stomach that someone would inflict harm on another being like this piece of shit had done to his woman.

Like her shoulders, Helena's entire body was bruised, clear finger and hand marks could be seen, along with long, deep scratches obviously made with scalpels and other sharp objects. Her fingers were distorted; clearly broken, and missing all fingernails. Callum sucked in a breath as he looked at her swollen stomach, swollen from the large incision bisecting it, red and inflamed.

"Did you do this?" Callum looked up and caught the eye of the doctor as he placed the sheet back over his bonded. Rage like nothing he had ever felt before welled up inside of him, ready to burst free at any moment.

"Did you?" he repeated as his hands flexed. He wanted to snap the neck of the male in front of him, break him like he had done to Helena.

"You will fucking die for what you have done, you and those that serve you." Callum stepped forward, his gaze fixed on the small human male. His hands clenched and unclenched. The room had become deathly quiet. The guards had quickly fallen to the skill of his brothers and none remained alive. None deserved to be.

They had given the right to mercy up the moment they had become a part of the evil that had taken place here. Before Callum had realised, he had his hand fixed around the doctor's throat. He could feel his heartbeat as it thundered against his hand. With every beat, Callum tightened his grip, eager to see the doctor's life slip away.

"Callum, stop, we will deal with this, with all of it. Your bonded needs you."

Callum slowly pulled his gaze away from the male to that of Sebastian. Understanding, not pity, peered back at him. Rage still burned through him, egging him on, that voice in the back of his mind telling him to exact revenge on the creature that had harmed the one thing that was good in his life: his pure, beautiful mate. But another part of him agreed with Sebastian. This wasn't his task. His task was now to look after Helena, heal her and bring her home. Callum nodded to his brother. "You will do this for me, Sebastian? You will make this right?"

"Yes, I swear it," Sebastian replied, right hand clenched into a fist, pressed to his heart. Callum nodded again, acknowledging the promise and bond Sebastian had just made. He released his hand from around the doctor's throat and turned, not giving him another glance. Everyone else in the room was forgotten as he pulled his dagger from under his jacket. Swiftly, he pressed the blade to his lower lip, creating a small gash in the flesh, letting the blood run freely before he bent over Helena. Slipping a hand under her head, he lifted and pressed his now bloody lips to her own, forcing her mouth open and, in turn, forcing the blood into her mouth.

What he was doing was against all succubi traditions. He was, in essence, forcing a bond with Helena, but it was the only thing he could think of to try and save her. His own life force would be joined to hers. He would feel her pain and hopefully, she would draw from his strength as a mate should.

Callum dreaded finding out what had been done to her. He dreaded the anger that would threaten to take over when he did find out.

He kept his lips against hers, letting his life force bond with hers before he felt that tug on his soul. Faster than he expected, Helena stirred. He felt, as well as heard, her whispered moan as she wrapped her arms around his neck. She gently licked at his lips and inside Callum celebrated a small victory as she recognised her soulmate. Keeping her covered by the sheet, he lifted her into his arms, shocked at how light and fragile she felt; her weight nearly halved by her incarceration. Without a backward glance, Callum stalked out of the exam room and passed the carnage his brothers and himself had done. Carnage that had been deserved.

It was time to get his mate home where she belonged.

12

Let the healing begin.

It had taken little time to travel back to the portal that would lead Callum home. He would ignore succubi ruling and take Helena straight to his own rooms, housed in a separate wing of the palace the succubi council and royal family used. The enforcers were the warrior force of the race and had to be housed together, as well as close to those they protected.

Since the immortal races had decided to hide themselves away from the mortals, they had been obligated to come to a truce. Being in such close proximity to creatures like vampyres, dark fey and demons of different lineage made for interesting neighbourly battles.

Each had been gifted with an area specifically for their race, there were boundaries and rules had been made. Each were also in charge of their own portals that were spaced out over London, hidden beneath every church. They could also open up in any city around the world, depending on the immortal's choice.

The succubi portal was based under the church at Whitechapel. The stunning white building shone in the street lights and called Callum home. He walked down the few stairs at the back of the church and approached the non-descript door. Holding Helena a little closer, looking again at her face, she had settled into a deep sleep after he had given her his blood, her heartbeat now steady and strong compared to the weak flutter it had been.

"Aperio" His deep voice echoed through the night, the old Latin word for open flowed off his tongue. The wooden door dissolved, leaving only a shimmering portal, one that rippled like the surface of a pond. After a quick check around, Callum confirmed he was alone before he stepped through and into the immortal realm. The sky above remained a deep blue, never changing, unlike the mortal realm. Shimmering in its depths were what looked like stars when, in fact, they were celestial beings that chose this realm to occupy. Always constant, never changing, a little like the immortal races themselves.

"We are home, baby," Callum bent his head and whispered to her, not sure if she would hear him or if he was just talking to himself. He would do whatever it took to bring her back.

Callum nodded to the guard that stood sentry over the gates to the palace and headed towards the enforcers wing. He would get Helena settled before he told the council she had been found.

Although the sky remained the same, it was classed as the middle of the night in their realm, so most would be asleep. For this he was grateful. He didn't want them asking what had happened to Helena, how had she survived. These were questions he wasn't ready to answer. He wanted answers himself, but that would take time.

She needed to heal and only the gods knew how long that would take.

Callum made it through the enforcer's wing with no one to stop him. Once he made it to his room, he quickly entered and made a beeline for the bed.

Holding her light form with one arm, he stripped back the bed before he laid her gently down. Every time he looked upon her face, his heart ached. His blood, although powerful, had brought the colour to her cheeks and had reduced the swelling to her face, but the other cuts, bruises and wounds would take a lot more to heal.

Callum brushed his fingertips gently down her cheek before he pulled the duvet up to her chin, tucking it tightly around her. Once done he walked back to his door, locking it and pressing the ring button on the intercom.

A tired but deep voice answered within two rings, "Albert speaking."

"Al, sorry it's..." Callum stopped, was it early or late?

"Callum, your back. Did you...?"

"Yeah, she's here. It's bad, Al. I'm going to need your help with this."

"How bad, what have you done so far?"

Callum could hear the enforcers' healer get dressed as he talked, could hear as he packed his bag. Albert had been the healer for hundreds of years and took zero shit from any of them, even the high council. Callum would trust no one else with the welfare of his mate and, if he was honest, he was reluctant to let even him see her in her current state.

He wasn't ashamed of her - that was the furthest thing from his mind. But every time he looked at the damage that had been done, he felt a sense of overwhelming guilt - that it was his fault this had been done.

"Callum!" Albert shouted over the intercom. "How bad is it?"

"Just get here and see for yourself."

Callum ended the call and walked back to the bed. How would he start to even contemplate healing her? How does one come back from this kind of torture, and if he was successful, would she still want him?

He sure as hell wouldn't blame her hating him. After all, it was his fault for putting her in the situation in the first place.

Pulling her hand from underneath the covers, he stroked her battered skin before he placed a kiss to each finger, wincing when he saw every single nail had been removed.

The pain she must have endured was mind numbing. Most enforcers would have broken under the strain.

"Helena, please forgive me," Callum whispered. "I'm sorry."

13

Choice! What choice?

The loud , reverberating knock at the door pulled Callum from his thoughts of guilt. Tucking Helena's hand back under the covers, he went to the door. Opening it, he expected to see Albert, only to be met by the furious face of Helena's minder, Mirium.

"Mirium."

"So, you're back then," she said angrily and pushed into the room, before she rushed to Helena's bedside.

"Oh, my sweet, sweet angel. What did they do to you?" she cried out.

Leaving the door unlocked but shut, Callum walked over to the bed.

"Are they dead, warrior?" It took Callum a moment to realise what the minder was asking, a moment she wasn't willing to give. "Well, did you avenge Helena or did you leave them alive to perform this atrocity to someone else? Are you the warrior I believed you to be?"

Her words cut deep but also brought anger back to the

forefront of his mind. She was a minder, who was she to question him as a warrior, as a mate?

"How dare you." Callum walked around the bed, growling as he went.

"How dare I?" Mirium growled back. "I dare alright, look at her, Callum!"

"I have looked, do you think I wouldn't? Do you think I don't care?" He started to shout, his own feelings bursting free. "I wanted to rip that doctor apart, piece by piece. I wanted to take pleasure in causing him as much pain as he had caused her."

Callum sat on the bed and again took Helena's hand, stroking the knuckles with such gentleness, it felt foreign.

"And?" the minder asked, "Did you?"

"No," he answered honestly, "I didn't, I left that task and honour to Sebastian and immediately brought her home." He paused, his eyes never leaving her sleeping face. "She is more important to me then my vengeance."

"Good." The minder nodded and bent over Helena, tears welling in her eyes. "Sebastian will make good on his word, you know how he feels."

Callum nodded in agreement, "Yes."

Silence filled the room as Callum sat and focused upon the feel of his fingers as they slid against the skin of Helena's knuckles. As much as he begrudged Mirium's presence, it would have been wrong of him to have kept her in the dark about Helena's rescue. The woman was like a one person spy team, she knew everything even before it happened. But she had given Helena a home and brought her up as her own.

"Callum." Her voice serious and no longer emotional called to him. He lifted his head and met her gaze.

"Why is there dried blood on her lips?" she asked, and Callum answered honestly.

"That's my blood, Mirium." He stood, he needed to be active and maybe giving Helena a bath would help his sudden irritability.

"Your blood," she gasped. "Do you know what you have done, what you have possibly started?"

"I had no choice," Callum fired back. "She was dying. I did what I had to, to save her life."

"Dying... What did they do to her?"

"I would like to know that, too, trust me. I am well aware I have forced a bond with her but I would rather that than the alternative."

"I understand, Callum, but if you have sent her into her maturity before you are officially bonded then you run the risk of her rejecting you. If she doesn't accept you or your bond then she could become dangerous."

"I know, but I don't know if they..." Callum couldn't say it.

"Raped her," Mirium finished. "If they did then the bond will be all the more difficult to cement in place."

Callum left the minder watching over his mate and moved to the bathroom. Turning the taps on, he started filling the tub, mindful not to make it too hot so as not to shock her system. He grabbed soaps from the cupboard and soft towels. If anything, he would make sure she was clean. He also wanted to see how bad the damage actually was. What if she had been raped? She wouldn't let him near her if that was the case, and then they wouldn't ever be bonded. If there was no bond and Helena became the monster most feared, then it would be up to him to put her down.

Could he do it, though? Could he kill the one person he loved? In the time she had been missing, Callum had realised once and for all that he loved Helena more than life itself. She was the air he breathed, his sun. Dammit, she owned his heart and soul, so to kill her would be to sentence himself to death.

He would take the afterlife, anyway. As long as it was by her side.

14

HEALERS KNOW IT ALL. OR DO THEY?

"Callum," Albert's voice called out to him, drawing him from his internal musings. His mind had drifted. It couldn't be helped, not with the current situation. He walked out of the bathroom quickly, to the healer who had just arrived. Only to find a standoff was taking place, a standoff between Albert and Mirium.

"What is she doing here?" Albert growled out, his voice irritable as their gazes clashed and held. The atmosphere felt thick and tense. In any other situation, it would have lightened Callum's current mood. Whatever was going on, there was certainly a long back story.

"What do you mean, what am I doing here? I have more bloody right to be here than you do." Mirium huffed and folded her arms across her chest, planting her feet in front on the bed, refusing to move.

"I couldn't give a shit what you think, but you need to

move, woman, so I can do my gods be damned job," Albert fired back.

Callum was unsure what had caused their ongoing rift, but he wouldn't put it past it being Albert's fault entirely. The ex-enforcer had a tendency to put his foot well and truly in it.

"Mirium, he's here to check on Helena, I asked him to," Callum explained, which only garnered him a sharp glare, before she reluctantly stepped to the side and allowed Albert to pass her.

"Fine," she snapped before a tense silence filled the room. Albert made a point of ignoring her as Mirium shot daggers into his back and Callum stood looking at both of them, wondering if they knew how silly they both actually looked. You could like it to school yard antics and this wasn't the time for it. Helena's wellbeing came first, above whatever petty differences they had with each other.

"Mirium," Callum said, his voice was stern but he didn't have time for her to be stomping around, acting like she had been deliberately put out.

"What?" she snapped and finally turned from watching Albert. Callum didn't respond and only looked at her, her bad attitude wasn't going to help Helena and she knew it.

"Fine," she huffed and walked towards the door. "I will go prepare some food." Mirium nodded to herself and reached for the door handle. Before she opened the door, she looked at Callum. "Thank you, warrior, for bringing her home."

Tears shone in the dim light of the room as Mirium smiled sadly, looking fondly on at Helena as the doc was examining her hands. Then she opened the door and left.

Instead of the expected slam, Mirium closed the door quietly, surprising them both.

"One day, old man, you will have to tell me what you did to piss her off."

"Ha! That story would take far too long and I am far too sober to retell it."

"That bad, eh?" Callum questioned, only receiving a smile in return. In that easy smile, Callum could see the playboy and rogue the healer had been known to be. Rumours had flown around, warning many a female to keep clear.

"Blessed goddess!" Albert hissed out. He had slowly removed the duvet covering Helena's body and had now revealed the damage that had been done. With the gentlest of touches, he reached over and took her chin, moving her head from side to side before he started to test the small burn wounds that had been caused at her temples. He probed the raw and oozing skin before he moved to check the other raw wounds. Every now and again, Helena's brow would furrow and a small moan would erupt from her lips, but she didn't wake.

"What caused those?" Callum asked, not liking the burns and shaved head on his mate. Her face looked so pale and gaunt compared to how she used to look.

"Shock therapy. The humans used to be fond of that kind of therapy for the insane back in the 1900's." Albert shook his head, taking in each and every bruise and cut Helena had. "These will all need to be documented. I just hope your brothers didn't destroy everything."

Callum frowned, why would anyone want to keep anything from that hellhole of a place? He hoped Sebastian had burned it to he ground. "I hope they wiped it off the face of the earth."

"You may say that now, Callum, but inside that place

may be evidence of what exactly they were doing. What they found out."

"I couldn't care less. We know what they were doing, Helena is proof that. They were evil and needed destroying."

Callum found himself filled with rage all over again. He growled out loud as Albert moved his examination down Helena's emaciated body. She was his mate, only he should be allowed to gaze at her unclothed.

"Callum, I suggest you either leave or get a grip, you know there is nothing I enjoy about this exam."

The healer was right, but that didn't stop every protective urge coming to life and wanting an outlet.

"Sorry," he mumbled and moved around to the opposite side of the bed, needing to be close to Helena but far enough away from Albert that he wouldn't throttle him.

"Callum, grab my bag from by the door, please?" Albert asked. Callum quickly did his bidding, placing the bag by his side and peered over his shoulder. The large wound across Helena's stomach was bright red in colour, the skin swollen. Each staple that had been placed to keep the flesh together now had a yellowish puss that oozed. Every time Albert palpated the area, more seeped out of the holes made by the staples and the smell of rot filled the room.

"Pass me the pliers that are in the side pocket and fetch a towel. I'm also going to need hot water, too."

"I've run a bath, will that help?" Callum asked as he dug out the pliers as requested and waited for the healer to answer.

"Yes, that may help. Ok, before that we are going to have to remove these staples and I'm going to have to deal with the infection. This is going to hurt her, Callum, so be prepared."

Callum nodded and moved towards Helena's head.

Taking her bruised and battered hands in his own, he kissed each finger. As soon as Albert started to pull on the staples, Helena's body thrashed, her back bowed and she screamed out. She still remained unconscious, as though she was trapped in whatever dream she was having at the time.

"You are going to have to hold her down," Albert said. Callum nodded and moved quickly. Sliding a hand under Helena, he moved behind her and wrapped his arms around her arms and chest. Resting his chin on her shoulder, he whispered in her ear.

"Shh, baby, it's ok. I've got you." Her body slowly calmed, surprising both of them, so Callum continued to talk to her, all the while he watched the healer remove each staple.

"Don't stop, old man," Callum pushed as the healer paused.

"This is going to hurt her, Callum, I won't lie. The wound seems to be necrotising. The only reason she isn't dead from septicaemia is because you gave her your blood." The healer used the towel to wipe away the putrid smelling fluids that had erupted from the wound as soon as he had removed the first few staples.

"Just do it," Callum grated out. Helena's body had started to shake and a fine layer of sweat covered her skin. From Callum's new view point, he could see every single piece of damage that had been done, including the bruises that were obviously handprints. Her breasts were purple and had one large print across the right one. His rage rolled in his gut, the need to cause harm to those that had harmed his angel became almost unbearable.

"No one will ever hurt you again, baby. This, I vow."

15

CAN BLOOD HEAL THE MIND AS WELL AS THE BODY?

"Baby, shhh, it's ok, shhh," Callum cooed as he rocked Helena in his arms. It had been 24 hours since he had brought her home and she still had not stirred. Her eyelids continued to flutter as she fought against the dreams that kept her away from him. She would cry out, moan and even scream in her tortured coma. He had no idea if she could hear him at all, but that didn't stop him from talking to her. He spoke his heart and told her of the things he had been too cowardly to speak of before. Things that, if his fellow enforcers heard they would no doubt call him soft-hearted. He didn't care.

Callum worried that they had been too late. Albert had finished trying to repair the damage that had been caused to her abdomen, they had been lucky in that sense. If Helena had been left any longer, even feeding her succubi blood wouldn't have saved her from the infection that had started to take hold. Since she had returned, Callum had fed her five times, eager to give her the best chance of healing. Even if, afterwards, she rejected him and their bond, he would deal with it with honour. Their newly formed bond, although incomplete, had served its purpose in bringing her back from the brink and restoring her own succubi healing abilities. Her body had been pumped with so many drugs she had been more mortal and, as such, deteriorated quickly.

Callum pressed a kissed to her temple, feeling the scrape of the stubble on her recently shaved head. He remembered how thick and soft her long hair had been and how he had watched her braid it. He himself had spent many a time running his fingers through the locks, but now, he had no idea how long it would take for it to grow back. That was a minor thing, though, compared to what his mate was currently dealing with.

Albert, in his examination, had been ordered by the high council to document every injury that had been inflicted on her. They worried, along with the enforcers, that this wasn't a lone facility and there were, in fact, multiple ones, each delivering their own personal hell to those of the immortal community. Other factions would have to be told and a decision would have to be made on who would be the ones that would hunt down those responsible. This attack also meant any visits for a non-enforcer to the mortal realm would be off-limits. Their race was already too low in numbers to risk the ones left.

Callum was brought out of his inner musing by Helena as she started to shake, her body again physically reacting to the healing process. Callum just hoped his blood was pure enough to heal her. Every time he fed her, he would check her palm to check the mark. A hope of seeing it darken kept him going, but each time he became a little more disheartened.

Holding her a little tighter, he again kissed her forehead and stroked her arms. Mirium had helped him bathe her, washing away every bit of dirt and grime. Any evidence of her ordeal that could be removed by soap and water had washed down the plug hole. If only healing the rest of Helena was as easy, Callum thought. Seeing her so vulnerable made his heart ache, seeing how emaciated she had become had brought him to his knees as he had let tears fall from his eyes. Every single rib protruded from under the skin of Helena's ribcage, her hip bones looked stark against her pale skin. Mirium had continued to wash Helena, letting him have his moment of grief, and grief it was. Those monsters, in their archaic quest for knowledge, had destroyed a creature so innocent and pure, there was no return. He may have Helena back in body, but it would take more than a gift from the gods themselves to bring her back as she was. She was and always would be, changed, and Callum grieved for that carefree spirit that had captured his heart all those years ago.

As was his knew habit, Callum picked up one of Helena's hands, caressing the delicate, soft skin and kissing the still sore fingertips. This was where he felt completely helpless, no gun or sword could beat this foe, and he had to do what he for once wasn't very good at: wait.

His thoughts again turned dark as he thought of her captors. In all of their history, this had been the first time the mortals had had the balls to kidnap one of their females for the purpose of experimentation. That alone opened up the possibility that they now knew they were not the only predators on the planet, and that made it dangerous for all other creatures.

The humans, with no special gifts or traits of their own, would see this as only a threat. Seeing only evil in the races that had survived for centuries had, at one time, helped the progression of their race. They were a selfish species, happy to annihilate anything that hindered them, the domination of the planet knew no bounds and right now, Callum wanted to wipe every fucking one off the face of the Earth. They had begun their discrimination of the immortal races around the time of the Witch Trials, but back then they had only executed any they had felt weren't human, they had never kidnapped them. That was until Sebastian's bonded was taken one night, that had caused not only retaliation to the humans but also the vampyres, too, as it had been them that had taken the female. Their current truce was a tentative one, as Sebastian had vowed to destroy them all after he had been told of her kidnapping and death.

To a leech, a female succubi was a walking, talking high, one they could feed from for centuries without worrying about drinking them to death. The blood of the females was as addictive as a vampyre's bite and as such, after a vampyre had become bored of the female, they were left fighting their own addiction. Most who survived the feeding would end up taking their own lives as their minds fractured and broke. Even after the passing of time, Callum knew Sebastian still grieved hard for his lost female, and was also why he took Helena's kidnapping personally, vowing to help find her and bring her home.

"Callum," Helena's whispered voice called out, bringing Callum out of his dark thoughts. His heart raced as hope bloomed within.

"Helena, my love," he replied. Using his fingers, he tilted her chin, expecting to see her beautiful pale eyes, only they remained shut, her lids fluttering as her scream continued.

Her brows were furrowed as her hands started to clench. He watched as her chest started to heave in and out as whatever horrors she had witnessed replayed in her mind. Holding her tighter, Callum started to rock her in his arms once again. Words of love and encouragement fell from his lips.

"It's ok, baby. You are so strong, you can do it."

16

Words can sometimes hurt more than actions.

A loud, forceful thud of a fist against wood, echoed through the room, bringing Callum out of his doze. Reluctantly, he slid out from behind Helena, trying his best not to jostle or move her too much. Tucking in her unconscious form, he left only her head peeking above the duvet. He bent and pressed a kiss to her small nose.

The unwanted visitor persisted, this time knocking louder and, in turn, forcing a growl from Callum.

"Give me a goddamn minute." His voice husky from his nap, he padded on bare feet across the wooden floor to the door, before throwing back the locks and opening it.

"What!?" he questioned, only to regret his ire instantly when the visitor was revealed.

"Sebastian?" he questioned, this time with no annoyance in his voice.

"Sorry, Callum, I did not want to disturb you but I felt I needed to see you, sooner rather than later."

"No, I'm sorry for snapping, my friend."

Sebastian just nodded, then added, "How is she?" Like a

true gentleman and warrior, Sebastian made no attempt to look beyond Callum as he stood in the doorway.

"Still asleep, if you can call it that. It's more like a coma, a nightmare she is unable to escape from. She cries out and sometimes you can see the pain on her face, yet nothing we've done has worked to bring her out of it," Callum admitted. Sebastian was the one male that would understand the loss of a bonded.

"I'm sorry, my friend." Callum nodded and looked back over his shoulder to Helena's sleeping form. He watched as she twitched then moaned before she settled back down.

"You are lucky to have her return," Sebastian started, "Luck was on your side." Callum watched as pain and grief flashed across his friend's face, before it was hidden once again.

"I know, but I fear we still may have been too late," Callum admitted again.

"Believe in your bond, Callum. But trust no one." Sebastian grew more intense, his gaze boring into Callum's, signifying the importance of what he had to say, "Michael knows about the return and also about you feeding her. He knows no official bond has taken place and if she turns, he's already put an order out to terminate her."

Callum was stunned at the news. They had only just returned and the chance of Helena turning when she was still in a coma was slim.

"How do you know this?" Callum asked, looking beyond Sebastian to the corridor, expecting to see the council guard.

"I overheard one of the guards. Just be careful, my friend, but know the alphas protect our own."

"Thank you, my friend."

"Another thing..." Sebastian stepped closer, sliding a recorder into Callum's palm "This may help you to understand what was done to your mate. The healer has a copy, but not the council. Just pray that Michael finds something else to occupy his warped little mind."

"Again, thank you, my friend."

Sebastian stepped back, placed his right fist at his heart and bowed before he turned to walk down the corridor, but Callum called out to stop him. He needed confirmation.

"Sebastian, did you?" he left the question unfinished, knowing his fellow enforcer would know what he was asking. Sebastian stopped and turned only his head, a slight tilt was the only other movement.

"It has been done." With that said, he walked away down the corridor, leaving Callum to stare at the black recorder in his hand.

Through the little window, he could see the small silver disc in place. All it would take would be the click of a button and the secrets of Helena's ordeal would be revealed. He was torn, torn between knowing exactly what had happened to his mate and not wanting to know, scared of what he would do when he found out. It created a pull deep inside Callum that twisted his gut and made his whole body tense. The damage that covered her entire body had been a culmination of months of abuse. It wasn't just on the outside, but the inside as well. Albert, in his sharp-toothed way, had hit the nail on the head when he had said, "healing her body was the easy part, the fight would be to heal her mind".

In the short period of time she had been with him, she had responded positively and rapidly to him feeding her. After each passing hour the bruises had started to colour then heal, scratches turned to scars and faded, too, only she didn't wake.

Shutting the door, once again Callum locked it, not trusting the guards now that Sebastian had told him their secret. Dimming the lights, he walked over to his dresser and pulled out a pair of headphones, plugging them into the recorder. He may want to hear what her captors had done, but there was no way in all the realms of hell he would let Helena, even unconscious, hear it. Brushing a palm across her pale cheek, Callum bent and kissed her lips before he moved over to the armchair at her bedside. Resting back in the leather, he placed the ear buds into his ears, Callum finally then gave in to the urge to click the play button. Sitting back in the chair, he listened, the voice of the doc coming through clear, making Callum's palms slick with sweat and his heart rate double. This was the bastard that had hurt his mate. This was the man that had, by the will of his gods, suffered with no mercy for his evil deeds.

"Subject 12 was brought in today after being followed along Oxford Street. In appearance she looks human, but nothing this beautiful can be."

Callum let his mind drift as he took in every word the doc relayed to the recorder, losing himself to the horrors his love had endured.

17

EVEN WARRIORS CRY

Callum's unconsciousness was filled with violence, torture and pain. He stood watching as the doc performed his tests on Helena, stood by, helpless, unable to stop it from happening, even as she called out his name, begging him to come for her. Every procedure she had been subjected to fired past his vision as if it had been put on fast forward like and an old VCR. Her screams echoed in his head, branded there forever, and still he stood, transfixed.

He watched as the doc killed his mate, unable to move. Watched as he brought her back, each time destroying her soul. He saw defiance in his mate's eyes before the end, watched as she boldly stated her hatred of a man that had taken so much from her in such a short period of time. Then Callum's dream was done, he was thrust back into the present with only the overwhelming feelings of guilt and disgust at himself to keep him company.

He tugged the ear phones free and sat up in the leather chair. Helena was exactly where he had left her, tucked under the covers; safe. Letting the recorder slip to the floor, he stood and walked to her bedside. After his nightmare, he wanted to see her in the flesh, make sure she was here and not back on that exam table. Emotions assaulted him, combinations of anger, pity, guilt and pride ate at him, pounding him from different angles.

Sebastian had been right when he had said he needed to hear what was on the recorder, only a part of him wished he hadn't. Every single test that had been done to Helena had been recorded. She had been treated like a specimen; only kept alive to study.

It sickened him whenever he thought of that male. No, he wasn't a male; males didn't do that to females. That man was evil. Callum shuddered as he remembered the enjoyment in the doc's voice as he relished every single bit of pain he inflicted.

Sitting on the side of the bed, Callum stroked his fingers down Helena's cheek. Ever since he had returned with her, he had been unable to take not touching her for longer than a few minutes. Feeling her warm skin against his hand, reminded him that she was, in fact, alive - broken, but alive. It ate at him that he had lost her. He was an enforcer, one of the best and a member of the alpha team. He was supposed to protect their race, yet the one that should be protected at all costs has been lost.

"Helena!" he whispered, "I'm sorry, baby, I let you down." His voice broke. "I would move the seven levels of hell to make this right," he vowed, and for the second time since he had brought her home, Callum sobbed.

"I know you hate me - fuck, I hate myself for letting this happen to you." He took a few deep breaths before he continued, "Come back to me, please," he pleaded as he cupped Helena's cheek and pressed kisses to her lips before he rested his head on her shoulder as he let the sobs overtake him. Letting everything he had kept locked deep within, out. Yes, he was a warrior, but he was still a creature with feelings and losing Helena had broken him in a way nothing else could.

"You are my light, Helena. I'm in the dark without you. Please, come back."

18

DEMONS DO EXIST, EVEN IN THOSE WE LOVE

The constant beeping of Callum's watch alarm woke him from his doze. He had been advised by Albert that Helena would need to be fed every few hours to help with the healing process. She also needed a strong dose of antibiotics to help her immune system battle the infection that had been caused by the doc's treatment. So he set an alarm that would keep him on track. This time, he had fallen asleep next to Helena not long after the last feeding and, yet again, he woke to her in the same condition.

Sitting up, Callum carefully extracted the pre-filled syringe from the box the healer had provided and, as instructed, injected the liquid into Helena's neck. It was the only place he could think to do it without making himself feel like the evil doc.

Placing the now empty syringe back into the box, Callum then reached for the small knife he kept by the bedside. Slicing across his lip and feeding Helena had become the easiest way to get his blood into her. Her body had responded as they had hoped and now only yellow bruising and faint scars remained from her ordeal. Even her hair had grown an inch, which now looked like it would grow back just as thick and glossy as he remembered.

Sliding the blade edge across his lip - as was his habit now - he moved to kiss his mate, only to find her eyes wide open. Hope bloomed within - she was awake.

"Helena?" he whispered and smiled down at her.

Her eyes just stared up at him. There was no facial expression as she looked up at his face, then her eyes flicked to his bleeding lip. Her eyes dilated at the sight of his blood and then moved to look at his hand that still held the knife.

"Baby?" he asked again, wanting Helena to say something, needing to know she was ok. Her gaze lifted and their eyes connected once again.

Her eyes were no longer the pale orbs he loved to look into. They were now a dull, dirty red that flowed over even the whites of her eyes. Her breathing had changed, her chest heaving with every breath, and Callum realised the gods had not looked kindly on them; he had been too late.

His mate, his love, had turned.

With no warning, Helena attacked and Callum let her. Releasing the knife into her own hand, he didn't mutter a word, never made a sound as he felt the blade slam through flesh and into his shoulder, driving straight through to the bone as Helena pushed him onto his back. Her naked form straddled him as she stabbed him again in the shoulder, releasing a torrent of blood that covered them both and fed her demon.

This was why the males bonded with the females before maturity. Not to protect the females, but to protect everyone else.

Helena fed and Callum did nothing to stop her. This was his fault, he had created this demon when he had failed to protect her. He would take his fate and death like a true succubi warrior.

"Take it all, my love, take it all," he breathed out, closing his eyes. Helena threw her head back and screamed in pleasure as she took his life's blood.

19

Not all tales end with a happily ever after

Callum ached all over, every muscle felt sore and he had shooting pains travelling up his shoulder and down his arm. His mind felt fuzzy and he struggled to simply open his eyes.

"Callum, you back with us?" a deep voice called out, and he forced his eyelids open. He winced as the light from his bedside lamp filtered into the orbs, causing pin pricks of pain to shoot through his skull.

"Dominic?" Callum questioned, confusion making him frown.

"Thank the gods," he heard Dominic breathe. "What's the last thing you remember?"

Moving to sit up, Callum groaned as his body protested. His mind tried to recall memories of before, but was only able to bring up fuzzy images.

Gently, he shook his head as he looked at the leader of

the enforcers. He had known Dom a long time, yet, even now, Dom looked uncomfortable.

"What happened?" he croaked out, and he couldn't miss the flash of pity that made a brief appearance on his face before it was hidden. Still, Dom said nothing, and that worried Callum.

"Dom, I know you aren't a coward, so out with it," Callum growled as he leaned back against the cushions of the bed. He was still in his room, but something seemed missing - different from before - but he couldn't quite put his finger on it.

"Listen, Callum, you've been through a lot," Dom started, his eyes wouldn't meet his and that bothered Callum. In everything they had been through, never once had Dominic not been honest with him. "We found you three days ago, unconscious and nearly dead. You had been bleeding out from two stab wounds in your shoulder."

Callum's eyes went wide and his hand crept up to touch his right shoulder, it was tender to touch and only a small scar remained.

"Can you really remember nothing?" Dominic asked again.

Callum looked down at his hand as he tried his best to focus on what could have happened. He fought to make the fuzzy images clearer. Pale eyes stared back at him from his mind, calling him and firing his memories into order.

Blood, acceptance and love.

His beautiful mate had turned, he had failed.

"Helena," he breathed and his eyes met Dominic's. Now the pity made sense. "Where is she?" His heart rate accelerated. "Where's Helena?"

"Callum, calm down."

"NO!" he shouted, "Where the fuck is she?"

Dominic stood and Callum jumped out of his bed, ignoring the wave of nausea and dizziness that nearly toppled him.

Dominic's eyes widened as Callum stalked him. He took a few steps back before he stood his ground. "Callum, she is alive, that is all you need to know."

"Where the fuck is my mate, Dominic?" Callum screamed, "Don't you dare take her from me!" Callum knew he was sounding unreasonable and most likely out of his mind. But the thought of Helena in anyone else's care but his, brought every single protective instinct he had to the forefront.

"Callum, she tried to kill you," Dominic calmly stated back. "She wasn't the Helena you remember, she is lost to us."

"NOOOOOOOO!" Callum fell to his knees, his face in his hands. Any sort of hope he had, had vanished, leaving only despair behind. He wished she had killed him, because his heart wasn't just broken, it was destroyed. It was a useless husk now, no use to him or anyone.

"My friend, I am truly sorry," Dominic's voice called from near his bedroom door.

"Get out," was all Callum could muster. He didn't even look up, only looked down at his hands, once again tracing the light pattern on his right hand. He had been so close, so close to having her back in his life and giving her everything she deserved.

Callum ignored the door as it opened and closed, signifying Dominic's leave. Callum wasn't bothered that he had shouted - even threatened - his mentor and leader. Instead, his focus was on his memories as they flooded back. The care and attention he had given Helena, the hope that she would come back to him as she slowly healed and the agony at realising she had turned. Her dirty blood red eyes had made her look like the demon of nightmares, and before he had blacked out, he had heard the pleasure in her scream as she fed from him. That was not his Helena, and yet, there was a huge part of him that refused to give up on his love. Although she was now doomed to a death sentence, his mind continuously turned over on how he could make things right.

Callum was unaware of how long he sat on the floor to his bedroom, wasn't aware what time of day it was. Only the cool touch of Sebastian's hand on his shoulder brought him out of his daze.

"Callum?"

Callum didn't answer.

"Callum, my friend, it is time to get up."

Callum ignored Sebastian, not wanting to move.

"My friend, if you have any hope of saving your mate, I suggest you get off your arse." Sebastian's stern voice filtered through his brain, reminding him of his days as a trainee and the beating he used to get for not listening to instruction. He lifted his gaze to meet the hardened one of Sebastian's.

"I've lost her."

"You will if you stay sat here."

Callum frowned.

"Get up," Sebastian urged, "Get up now."

"But, how? She's turned."

Sebastian was already at the door, collecting Callum a top from the chair on his way, launching the material at Callum before he peeked out the door. "There may be a way, but you need to hurry. The council will not spend long discussing when to execute her. You've lost three days already."

Callum threw on the t-shirt, slipped his feet into his Nikes left by the door and followed Sebastian out of his room.

He didn't talk. Instead, he waited for Sebastian to reveal more. His brain was a mess of information and Callum wasn't sure how much more he could take.

"Listen, you had already started a bond before Helena was taken."

Callum stopped. "How did you...?"

"I just know," Sebastian said with a small smile. "Because of this, there may be a chance that a full bonding will work."

"A full bonding? I love her Sebastian, but she did try to kill me. How the fuck am I going to be able to have sex with her?"

The elder warrior said nothing, but continued down the corridor towards the oldest section of the palace. This was where the enforcers' training rooms were housed and where their makeshift dungeons were stationed. Usually, they didn't need holding pens for the guilty as most were killed in the battle, as was the immortal way. No point in keeping alive a being that would most likely escape at some point.

Callum became angered at the thought of his delicate, beautiful mate caged up like an animal, only to realise, at this moment in time, she was in fact more demon than woman. Myths and legends spoke of how dangerous succubi women were before the males had found a way to tame them. Hundreds, if not thousands, of men had perished to the will and whims of succubi females, whose blood lust and sexual appetites were never sated.

Thoughts filled his mind of how the males of old had first calmed their females, how they had controlled a being that, in the demon state, was stronger than any male. Callum had almost died once, but when he thought about it, being without Helena would be worse than dying. He would gladly give his life for hers.

That's what they would have vowed to each other if the bonding ceremony had taken place. His vow to always protect and be the key that would keep her soul safe had been first and foremost in his mind. He would do everything he could to bring her back, and if not, then the council could put him to death right next to her.

As Sebastian stopped outside the door that would lead underneath the training level, he looked Callum in the eye. "This isn't going to be easy, my friend."

Callum laughed, but it felt hollow. He tried to stay upbeat, "Neither were your lessons, but I managed."

Sebastian returned his laugh and held out his hand to shake Callum's own. "You always were my best, when you weren't being the smart-arsed student."

As Callum clasped palms with his fellow enforcer, the seriousness of the situation fired his blood.

"The alphas will make sure no one disturbs you, but we don't have a lot of time."

Callum nodded and reached out to grab the door handle.

"Do what you must, even if it seems wrong at the time."

"You mean force her, don't you?" Callum asked, looking his friend in the eye.

"She will not see it as such; it will be more along the lines of you forcing yourself." With a small grin, despite the direness of the situation, Sebastian turned, "But I'm sure you are more than *up* for the challenge."

"Lame, old man. Lame."

"Good luck, Callum. May the gods watch over you."

Callum watched as Sebastian walked up the corridor before he pushed through the door to the dungeons. The smell was old and damp, your stereotypical run of the mill dungeon that spoke of ages past and centuries old torture. If walls could talk, these would tell tales of blood and anguish.

Apt considering what he was about to attempt.

His feet made barely a sound as he moved down the stone steps. The only light came from traditional torches, their smell reminding Callum of his youth and helping to clear his still foggy mind.

As he stepped into the main room, chains could be heard slamming against the stonework as screeches and cries of anger echoed off the walls.

Steeling his shoulders, Callum approached the cell on the far left, the thick steel bars separating him from his now turned mate. Dressed in nothing but one of his t-shirts, she stared back at him from beyond the bars. Her eyes, now bright red, fired anger and then lust in his direction. Small fangs could be seen pressing into her lower lip that was coated in blood. Her bare arms sported new bruises and bite marks from where she had started to bite her own arms in desperation. In her hands she held the chains that meant she could move no more than four feet from the wall. It had been those slamming against the wall that he had heard.

Helena was not happy.

"Baby?" he questioned as he stepped up to the bars.

His answer came as a hiss as Helena moved to run against the bars, only to be flung back as the chains held fast.

Her screech of annoyance filled the cell.

Walking to the cell door, he unhooked the padlock that he assumed Sebastian had unlocked and opened the door. Closing it behind him, Callum steeled himself for the battle that was to come. Helena now faced him, the chains no longer in her hands. Instead, they clenched and unclenched as her chest heaved.

It was a face-off, pure and simple, and there would only be one winner.

He had her attention, now all he had to do was man the fuck up and tame his mate.

20

Bonds can be broken. But can they be remade?

"Helena," he said, and held his hands out, palms up, in a non-threatening gesture. He both wanted and needed to get through to her. He wanted the bond complete, but he never thought he would have to force it in a dungeon.

It would surprise him if he could even get fucking hard, the whole thought of his mate trying to rip out his throat in a sex-filled, blood-crazed stupor actually hindered his libido, rather than enhance it.

Stepping closer still, he stopped within a foot of her reach, hating the sound of her screeches. This was not his mate, but she was in there somewhere and even if it killed him, he would find her again.

"Helena, my love, will you come back to me?" he asked in a soothing voice, coaxing as he stepped within range of her extended hands. Reaching up, he took hold of them in his own, holding on tight as she started to fight.

"Helena, in all of this, please remember that I love you with every breath in my body. Where you go, I go, baby."

As he took a hard grip of her hands, he forced them - chains and all - behind her back, pinning her against his chest, immobilising her, yet putting him in direct range of her clashing teeth. Callum made no sound of protest as she bit into his shoulder. Instead of making her fight more, it settled her down as she pressed her lips to the bite and fed.

Maybe this wouldn't be as hard as he expected. Feeling confident, he released her hands to move his up her body and around her shoulders, holding her head to him.

"That's it, baby, shhh," he cooed, and relaxed.

Helena's scream erupted first and once again Callum found himself flat on his back with his mate straddling him. Her strength and agility surprised him, as did the speed with which she shredded his shirt, leaving his chest bare for her nails. She screeched again as she moved against his groin. With no underwear on her, he could feel her heat and as she bent her head and bit into his chest. He responded as he thought he never would.

Using her distraction to his advantage, he thrust up against her, smiling a small victory when she groaned but kept feeding, her hips surging against his, riding his growing erection. Sebastian had been right; there would be no need for any force other than her will under his.

It was his battle to win.

Hooking a foot around hers, in one fluid movement he rolled them towards the wall, creating slack on the chains and making it possible for him to force Helena's hands above her head. She screamed and bucked under him, fighting to be free. Her eyes blazed with defiance, Callum had never seen Helena look so fierce. Leaving the thinking behind, Callum bent his head and took Helena's lips in a bruising kiss, forcing her mouth open and taking control. He asserted his dominance, making her bow to his rule. Unable to stop himself, Callum bit down on her lip, tasting blood, her blood sending his own senses sky rocketing. Groaning out loud, he sucked on the wound, drawing more of her essence into him even as his now hard groin settled against her heat.

"Fuck," he groaned again as she bit his lip in return. Her fighting had stopped. Instead, she clawed at his bare back, wanting him closer. Only his joggers blocked him from being inside her, but he refused to release her, just in case she fought back and escaped his hold, and that was not an option. Still he thrust against her, each moan and screech of pleasure egged him on as they fed from one another. Blood coated them both, yet still, she wasn't his Helena.

Callum growled out and pressed harder, his only goal now was release, to give her the best orgasm of her short life and maybe, just maybe, bring her home.

Biting into his own lip once more, he released more of his blood and then merged his and hers together.

One heart - one soul.

Live or die, they would be together - always.

21

SEBASTIAN

Sometimes hope can be the evil we try to escape.

Sebastian looked at his watch. Time had gone quickly since he had led Callum down the corridor to his fate. Whether the young enforcer would prevail was only for the gods to decide, but if he could help sway them in his favour, then he would.

He knew the task ahead would be one no one would have chosen, but it was, after all, the journey that made the destination all the sweeter to experience. If both Callum and Helena came out of this alive, they would have a bond so solid it would rival even that of the royals. Pushing himself upwards, Sebastian left the comfort of his own quarters, nodding to his fellow enforcers as he went. It was only Dom that stopped him.

"It's been only an hour?" he questioned, but fell into stride at his side.

"Yes it has, but I have a feeling the council will be coming soon so I dare not wait any longer."

As he said this, multiple footsteps could be heard entering the dungeons. They were out of time.

Both continued towards the dungeons, neither knowing what to expect, worst case would be their friend would have gone out in a blaze of blood, but they both had hope.

Their steps echoed on the stone floor, but that was the only sound that greeted them as they walked into the chamber where the cells circled the room. There was no sound.1

Moving to stand in front of the last cell on the left, silence became their new friend. This, they had never expected.

22

CALLUM

Taking a chance, believing in love

Sweat coated Callum's chest, his breaths sawed in and out and his body ached like he had done a few hours lifting in the gym. That wasn't the case here; it was more like battle. He had been in a few in his life, but none had prepared him for the battle he had just won.

He raced up the back staircase that would lead to the enforcers' quarters. In his arms was an unconscious, yet, for now, sated Helena. He had refused to leave the dungeons the way he had entered. After what had occurred, there was no way in this realm or the next he would let any male look upon his mate. Sebastian and Dominic had entered, just as he had been about to leave, to warn him his time had been up. They had been true to their word and had warned him, at least giving him a little longer to cement the bond in place. There was still one part left to do and he would need Helena awake and responsive.

What a beautiful sight she was. Even though they were both coated in the grime from the dungeon's floor, and their own blood, she still looked perfect in his eyes. Although his evening had started off dire, it was certainly looking up now. Callum had lost track of time, but whether it had been a few minutes or a few hours, all that mattered was that he had won. Although they hadn't resorted to full intercourse, the three orgasms he had wrung out of her had been enough to force her demon back. The issue was, he didn't know how long it would last.

Lifting her higher into his arms, he peeked his head out from the hidden doorway that was seldom used and looked up the corridor. With thanks to the gods and his fellow alphas, Callum stepped out and hurried towards his room. There was still the possibility that the council would show up and try to take Helena away again. Even though she had turned back, they would still be eager to interrogate her. Some - from what he had heard - felt that bringing her back would jeopardise the race and lead the humans to their realm. Callum couldn't care less what they thought; they would not be taking his mate away from him. He would get her clean, wake her up and then seal the bond like they were supposed to do. Unfortunately, blood and orgasms, no matter how many, were not enough. Words needed to be spoken, vows to be taken, before they would be bonded together.

"Callum." The deep voice calling from beside his door had Callum stopping. He tightened his grip on Helena as he faced both Dominic and Sebastian. It surprised him that they were waiting for him already but he had learned never to underestimate either of them. They had a knowledge and skill most warriors only dreamed of.

"Boys," Callum answered, but said nothing else. Instead, he growled as Sebastian stepped forward and lifted Helena's right hand that had slipped to the side. A feeling of intense hatred for Sebastian hit him square in the chest and he felt another growl rumble up his throat. Never in his life had he ever felt like this towards, not only his mentor, but his friend of many years.

"Easy, Callum." Sebastian growled back before he held her hand, looking at her palm. "That's the bonding taking effect," Sebastian answered his thoughts, making Callum feel like his mind was an open book.

"Back off," he growled again, tugging Helena's hand from Sebastian and turning his body, trying to keep her out of view of the warriors. He couldn't shake the feeling - the need - to keep her out of sight from any and all males, to claim his mate fully and mark her so everyone knew she was his.

Callum could feel his blood heating at the thought. Finally, after all this time. Helena had been his in word and oath since they were small but now, finally, she would be his in deed.

"My friend, you must hurry, we have delayed them for now," Sebastian urged, unaware of the emotions flowing through Callum and Helena.

"HALT!" a Royal guard called from around the corner as more followed, flanking their leader. Although there was no longer a Royal family in residence, the high councillor still kept their names. Some thought he hoped for the return of the monarchy where as others knew he wanted power for himself and kept the term as he felt he would become the next king.

"That female is under arrest and should be in the

dungeon." The leader glared at Sebastian and Dominic as they stood at Callum's side.

"The Female..." Callum sneered back, not at all happy with how they were talking about his mate, "Is fine and requires rest."

"But she has turned and is to be put to death," the leader fired back as the others drew their swords.

"Look for yourself. As you can see, she is no longer turned," Callum offered. Helena still said nothing, but looked at the guards. Her face devoid of emotion.

"But..."

Sebastian stepped forward and Dominic followed, putting themselves between the royal guard and Callum.. Doing what Alphas did best: protecting their own.

"As you can see, the female is fine and no longer a threat to the race," Sebastian said, voice stern yet quiet

"You Alphas are a law unto your own, the council shall hear about this, and you," the guard pointed at Callum, "don't expect to keep her, she has been marked." He smiled, the tilt of his lips cruel.

"You dare threaten a bonded?" Dominic intervened. "You dare threaten a warrior? Take your complaints, petty as they are, to the council, I will be giving my own report," Dominic threatened. Both Alphas stood their ground, watching until the Royal guard had left.

Callum nodded in thanks at his friends. Without them, he wouldn't have his mate back.

"Callum," her quiet voice whispered across his cheek. The two males forgotten, he looked down into Helena's pale eyes and became lost. Emotions that he too felt flashed across them, drawing him in.

"Shhhh, baby, it's ok, I got you." Without further thought to Dominic and Sebastian, he pushed through the entrance of his room, kicking the wooden door shut and engaging the lock before he walked over to his large bed. Gently placing Helena down on the duvet, he sat next to her.

Moments passed by as they just stared at each other, pale blue eyes meeting dark green and, for Callum, it felt like the world had stopped. With courage he never knew he had, he slipped off the bed and onto the floor, balancing on his knees.

Still, she never said a word.

Taking both her hands in his own – their size engulfing her smaller, more delicate ones - he turned them over so they were palm up, showing the now slightly darker mark on her right hand.

Still, she never said a word.

Bowing his head, he dragged his gaze away from hers and kissed both palms before placing his forehead in them.

Still, she never said a word.

"Helena, I ask you forgive me," Callum started and a lump formed in his throat. Although they had been through a partial bonding and she had been pulled back from being turned, Callum - if he was honest - expected Helena to reject him. He didn't want her to stay out of gratitude or some misplaced idea that she had a promise to keep.

He wanted her to bond with him for one reason and one alone: that she loved him as much as he loved her.

He loved her enough that if she decided here and now that she would walk away, even after everything, he would let her. He owed her that much at least.

"I know I am to blame for the ordeal you have been through, it is my fault that you have been hurt," he continued, keeping his head down, thankful she hadn't removed her hands from his grasp. The feel of her warmth centred him like no other. Even a partial bonding intensified his feelings tenfold, and they would only grow with time - unless she rejected him.

"Callum." His name on her lips, after all this time, was bliss to his ears. The amount of times he had laid awake at night, imagined hearing her voice, seeing her stunning face and touching her soft skin. Finally, she was here.

"Callum," she repeated, and he lifted his head to look into her eyes once again. Her smile was small, but she didn't pull away. That gave him hope, only her next words floored him:

"Heart of my heart,
Soul of my soul,
Together as one,
Always whole.
This male I take as my bonded,
This male I take as my own,
Bond us together for all time.
Always together, never alone."

Helena's soft voice spoke the ancient vow of the succubi bonding ceremony and Callum had frozen in place. He had expected rejection, not for her to initiate their joining. It took all of a few moments for Callum to locate his brain and respond, her frown had him stuttering on the words, trying to get them out before she changed her mind:

"Heart of my heart,
Soul of my soul,
Together as one,
Always whole.
This female I take as my bonded,
This female I take as my own,
Bond us together for all time,
Always together, never alone."

Without looking, Callum reached for a blade he always

kept hidden under the mattress. It was a habit and one he was now thankful for. Taking the steel, he swiped the sharp edge across his left palm and held it up. Helena had now sat up and watched him with that smile still on her lips. Still coated in blood and grime, she would always be the most beautiful creature to ever exist. A tiny part of Callum's mind rebelled when she gently took the blade from his hand - remembering the way she had attacked him – but that was soon out of his mind as she copied his actions. The blood welled in her palm before she lifted it up and pressed her left palm to his. Their fingers interlocked, blood mingling as they completed the vow together.

"Bonded with blood, bonded with love. By the gods will, let this be done."

Silence filled the room. In all honesty, Callum had expected the lights to blink and an unknown wind to rush through the room, letting them know the gods approved of their bond. But nothing happened.

He was glad.

The gods didn't need to tell him this was a good match; his heart did, and right now his heart was screaming for his mate.

"Helena," he breathed as he stood. Keeping her palm against her, he melded his lips with hers, putting every desperate feeling he had felt since her kidnapping into their kiss. Every feeling of loss he poured into the kiss and he knew she felt the same as her free hand delved into his hair. Her groan had him pulling back.

"Baby, you ok?" he asked, breathless as he pulled back. He was pleased to see she was just as affected as he was.

"Callum, you came for me, you saved me and you brought me back when I had no hope." Tears filled her eyes and it broke his heart all over again. He went to talk, but she placed her fingers over his lips. "You were with me," she admitted, "Every time I thought I couldn't go on, you were there."

"Baby..."

"You were, I remember everything, Callum, every bit of pain *he* caused, as well as the pain I caused." Helena touched Callum's shoulder, her fingers gently tracing the scars. "You came for me when I thought I was lost, that there was no way back from the dark chasm I found myself in. But then you were suddenly there, bringing me home. Saving my soul."

Tears now fell freely from Helena's eyes and Callum swiped them away with his thumb, as his own fell. The pain she had been through was unimaginable, yet, here she was, willing to forgive him.

"Callum it was never your fault that I was taken," she answered, echoing his thoughts, "It was no one's fault but those animals that took me." Taking both her hands, she cupped his cheeks.

"Callum, I love you," she stated simply and pressed her lips to his.

Callum wrapped Helena in his arms, pulling her tight to his body and lifting her off the bed. He felt her wrap her legs around him as their kiss deepened. Without breaking their kiss, Callum walked them towards the bathroom. As much as he needed her, they both weren't in any state for what he planned. He didn't want to break the kiss, but forcing his lips away, he smiled down at Helena's pouting face.

"We need a shower, baby," he admitted and her eyes widened as she finally realised how filthy they really were. Sitting her on the counter next to the shower, he moved and turned on the hot water before he started to strip out of his joggers, leaving the ripped material on the floor. Thanks to

Helena's earlier behaviour, his shirt had long since been destroyed.

Walking back to stand in front of her, his hands reached up and tugged the material of his t-shirt up and over her head. She showed no embarrassment as her body was revealed to him. Yes, he had seen it before, but not while she was awake.

"Err, yeah," she replied distractedly, her eyes moving up and down his own naked form. There was nothing but love and trust in her eyes.

"We have time, Callum." It took a second for him to realise what she was referring to and he smiled back, although his body had other ideas. He willed it to calm as she held out her arms for him. Picking her up into his arms, he walked into the large shower.

"We have all the time in the world, baby," he answered. They needed time to heal and to be in each other's arms before he did the honourable thing and made her his completely.

After all, it wasn't just the sex that made a succubi female so desirable, it was their unconditional love and their ability to forgive.

She was his, just as he was hers.

Bonded now and always.

This wasn't the end, only the beginning.

23

WITH DARK CONFUSION COMES DARK NEED
Dominic

"Enforcer, can you please clarify why the female..." The council member looked at the paper in front of him as he read the name, "Helena, is still alive and why she has not been executed, as per orders?"

Dominic looked at the Royal guard that stood behind the council member, eager to knock the smirk that was on his face, off. It was obvious the guard had done what he had suggested and reported the situation, only the guard wouldn't have that smirk for much longer. Dominic hated the council; they were pointless. The only reason they had ever had power over the race was because their queen had died, along with her consort and the only heir. But they hoarded whatever power they could get and didn't like it when anyone challenged them, least of all an enforcer they thought was too low and beneath them to matter.

Keeping his voice neutral, he answered, "Helena was rescued from the facility run by the humans, as reported. Due to the direness of her injuries, enforcer Callum, who had been set to bond with her, made the decision to start the bond to save her life."

Dominic ignored the whispers from the other members of the council as they displayed their disapproval at the enforcer's actions.

"But it didn't work, did it?" The question was fired at him and was laced with distaste.

"Yes, it did, councillor. Helena healed from her injuries. Their bond saved her life," Dominic countered, starting to lose his patience.

"But she turned!" The statement was said by none other than Michael, the high councillor, and one of the few people that irritated Dominic. Looking him in the eye, Dominic answered honestly, but refused to let these limp-wristed book-jockeys win. They wanted control of everything. Unfortunately for them, the enforcers, especially the Alpha team, were hard to control. The council needed them to protect the race. So, in short, they needed them a damn sight more than the enforcers needed the council.

"Yes, she turned, but Callum was able to bring her back by finishing their bond. Helena is now fully healed and fully bonded." Dominic spoke loud and clear, making them well aware that now Helena was bonded to one of his warriors, to try to punish her would be to start a rift with the enforcers. They protected their own and they would choose Callum and his mate over the whims of the council.

Michael sneered. They had never got on and Dominic really couldn't have cared less. Michael's opinions and ideas on how to rule their race was sketchy at best, and most didn't trust him. Most had no choice but to follow his lead.

"Dominic, as leader of the Alpha team we need you try and find out if there are any more of these "testing" facilities in London. We cannot risk more members of our race being taken. Take your men and scour the city. Can you do this, or should I ask one of the other teams?"

Dominic's fists clenched. In his mind, he was ramming them down Michael's throat. "Yes, we can do that, consider it already done." Dominic bowed, as was custom. The gesture used to mean great respect, but he had none for Michael. Turning on his heel, he walked out of the chamber. He hated doing what the council said, but with the mood he was in, he was up for a fight.

He had already promised Callum that if they found any other facility, he would grant him the honour of razing it to the ground. It was time to be the leader his enforcers expected; he just hoped it calmed his "other" side enough that he didn't murder a certain council member. That definitely wouldn't put him in the council's good books.

Pulling his phone out of his pocket, he dialled his second in command. "Bastian, it's on. Tell the team we leave in thirty."

It was time for the Alpha team to show why they were the best, the strongest, the most feared.

Why they were Alpha.

Dark Need- Dark Desires, Book 2

ALSO BY J THOMPSON

Soulmate Series

SoulKiss-http://soulmatenovels.com/soulkiss.htm

SoulFate-http://soulmatenovels.com/soulfate.htm

SoulDeath-http://soulmatenovels.com/souldeath.htm

Dark Desire Series

Dark Confusion-http://soulmatenovels.com/dark-confusion.htm

Dark Need-http://soulmatenovels.com/dark-need.htm

Trinity Series

Ebony-http://soulmatenovels.com/ebony.htm

Paranormal Security Service

Guarding Katelyn-http://soulmatenovels.com/guardian-katelyn.htm

Tears of Havoc

Cupid's Essence-http://soulmatenovels.com/cupids-essence.htm

Elemental Dragons Series

Earth Dragon's Claim-http://soulmatenovels.com/earth-dragons-claim.htm

Co-authored

Dragon fire and Phoenix Ash-http://soulmatenovels.com/dragon-fire-and-phoenix-ash.htm

Draakon Desire Series

Raanar-My Book

Stand Alones

Exercise in Love -http://soulmatenovels.com/exercise-in-love.htm

Magic and Mayhem Universe

Witch out of Water-Kracken's Hole Book 1-https://magicandmayhemuniverse.com/j-thompson/

Tail of a witch- Kracken's Hole Book 2-https://magicandmayhemuniverse.com/j-thompson/

Witch out of Luck- Kraken's Hole Book 3-https://magicandmayhemuniverse.com/j-thompson/

Altorian Cyborgs

Betraying Ko'ran- http://soulmatenovels.com/betraying-koran.htm

ABOUT THE AUTHOR

J. Thompson is a USA Today Bestselling Author of Paranormal and Sci-Fi romance and a major fan of procrastination. Jenn has always loved history, so using her wild imagination and tying in her love of history and fantasy, she began a new adventure into the world of words. Weaving romance into old worlds and giving life to her mythical inspired novels is what Jenn does best, and she has a lot more planned in the future, including some hard assed demons.

When she isn't bent over her laptop with the crazy writer eyes, you will find Jenn making jewellery, cross stitching and it doing paper crafts. Jenn is also an avid lover old skool skills like archery and sword fighting.

Maybe a touch nuts Jenn is an author who believes wholeheartedly that people are good and that everyone deserves romance - even Hades.

Connect with Jenn online at www.soulmatenovels.com
For regular updates sign up to Jenns Newsletter HERE

Printed in Great Britain
by Amazon